Dear Reader,

I really like the characers in *And the Desert Blooms*. I first introduced Pandora and Phillip in *A Summer Smile*. "Introduced" isn't quite the correct word. Even though they were secondary characters, I had trouble keeping them from dominating the book. I knew the moment I saw their interaction that I had to give them a book of their own. They were both strong, yet vulnerable, and the sparks flew.

I think you'll agree that those sparks developed into fireworks in *And the Desert Blooms*. All the ingredients were certainly present: sheikhs and show business and two people who were meant for each other and have to figure out a way to overcome odds to get there. I had a great time with them.

I hope you enjoy reading it as much as I did writing it.

Iris Johansen

Iris Johansen

IRIS JOHANSEN

~

And the Desert Blooms

BANTAM BOOKS

AND THE DESERT BLOOMS
A Bantam Book

PUBLISHING HISTORY
Loveswept edition published January 1986
Bantam mass market edition / January 2009

Published by Bantam Dell
A Division of Random House, Inc.
New York, New York

This is a work of fiction. Names, characters, places, and incidents
either are the product of the author's imagination or are used
fictitiously. Any resemblance to actual persons, living or dead, events,
or locales is entirely coincidental.

Bantam Books and the rooster colophon are registered trademarks of
Random House, Inc.

ISBN: 978-0-553-59230-6

Printed in the United States of America
Published simultaneously in Canada

www.bantamdell.com

OPM 10 9 8 7 6 5 4 3 2 1

ONE

PANDORA QUICKLY UNFASTENED the chain of the medallion that hung around her neck. Her hands were shaking slightly as she took it off and placed it in the velvet-lined jeweler's box. She took a moment to draw a deep, steadying breath. It was stupid to be so frightened now. She had planned everything down to the last detail. No, nothing could go wrong.

The round medallion shone against the black velvet lining of the box. The morning sunlight streaming through the hotel room window picked out the design on its surface, a raised rose in full bloom pierced by a sword. She reached out one finger and touched the rose gently. She felt oddly naked without the necklace she had worn for the last eight years. She had a sudden impulse to snatch the lovely thing out of the box and fasten it around her neck again. It was *hers,* dammit. What if Philip just opened the package and then carelessly tossed the medallion into a drawer?

What if he had forgotten her? It had been more than six years. Undoubtedly there had been a parade of women through his bedroom in that time. Perhaps he'd found one who could provide him with more than temporary satisfaction. Oh Lord, she mustn't think of that. It hurt too much. She *wouldn't* think about it. He wasn't married or engaged. She knew that for certain. It didn't matter if he had formed a liaison or not. She'd soon take care of removing any woman who had taken his fancy. Philip belonged to her. She had a prior claim and wouldn't hesitate to state it. She knew Philip better than anyone on the face of the earth. Surely that would be a powerful enough weapon to oust any rival. And she had other weapons now as well. She would use them all if she had to.

Philip wouldn't throw the medallion into a drawer. He was the most possessive man she had ever known. When he had given her this medallion he had done so as a gesture of ownership. What belonged to him would never be surrendered easily.

She snapped the box shut and reached for the most recent issue of *Rolling Stone* magazine. With efficient movements she wrapped the jeweler's box and the magazine in plain brown paper and addressed it to James Abernathy, Philip's London agent. From the gossip columns she knew Philip had spent a good deal of time in Great Britain during the last six years. Even if he wasn't in London, Abernathy would know where to reach him.

Just as she finished there was a knock on the door. She stood and snatched up the package and her huge shoulder bag from the chair beside the desk. "Just a minute," she called.

"Take your time," came Neal's deep voice. "I'm

in no hurry to listen to you destroy my new lyrics with that sandpaper voice of yours."

A smile tugged at her lips as she crossed the room, and she felt some of her tension ease. Neal Sabine's dry humor always had that effect on her. She couldn't remember how many performances he had made bearable for her in the past two years.

She threw open the door. "Then why don't you sing them yourself?" she asked Neal with a grin. "We both know you've got a better voice." She made a face. "Hell, Kermit the Frog has a better voice."

"But Kermit the Frog doesn't have your sex appeal," he replied as he took her huge shoulder bag and slung it over his shoulder. "And neither do I. You may not be melodious, but you're definitely commercial."

"Thanks a lot," she said. "If I was the least bit serious about all this nonsense, I'd probably be crushed."

"If you were serious, I wouldn't have said it," Neal returned. "I'd be working your ass off to make a musician out of you, instead of just a star." He shifted his guitar case and took her arm. "Come on, let's get on the road. Pauly and Gene are already at the auditorium rehearsing." One side of his mouth lifted in a lopsided smile. "They're obviously more driven than we are, luv."

She knew better than that, but said nothing as she closed the door and started down the hall toward the bank of elevators at the end of the corridor. "I'm afraid we're going to be even later than you think," she remarked finally. "I have to stop at the post office and mail this package."

There was a flicker of curiosity in Neal's eyes as he glanced down at the package. In the four years he had known Pandora he couldn't remember her either receiving or sending any mail. She seemed to live totally in the here and now. "I guess I can handle that. Is it important?"

"Oh yes, it's important." Her hand was trembling again as she pushed the button of the elevator. She deliberately steadied it. She mustn't be so transparent. She could tell by Neal's expression that he'd already noticed something was upsetting her. She'd never be able to fool Philip, who had always been extraordinarily sensitive to her emotional state, if she couldn't control herself better than this.

She lifted her chin and gave Neal a blindingly beautiful smile. "Very important." Her smile suddenly faded, and a faint frown creased her forehead. "Do you remember last year when you were ill with the flu and I played Florence Nightingale?"

He nodded. "How could I forget? I've never been so bitchin' miserable in my life."

"You said you owed me one."

His eyes narrowed. "Are you calling in debts, Pandora?"

She nodded. "I need a favor." She moistened her lips. Heavens, this was hard. She had taken care of Neal because he was her friend and he needed her. She felt shabby extracting payment now for what she had given freely. "I'll understand if you don't want to do it, but I thought I'd—"

"Oh, for heaven's sake, be quiet. Pandora." The doors of the elevator slid open and Neal nudged her into the cubicle. "You're my friend, dammit." His thumb punched the lobby button. "If you want a favor, ask. It's not a crime to need a little help, you know."

"Okay." She drew a deep breath. "I want you to move in with me."

"What!"

The doors of the elevator slid silently closed.

"Come in, Abernathy."

James Abernathy hesitated a moment before he opened the polished oak library door. He wasn't in any hurry to beard the lion in his den. He had deliberately taken his time getting to El Kabbar's estate from his office in London. Usually it annoyed him to make the long drive when the sheikh wanted to sign papers or relay instructions on the more delicate transactions of his multicorporation empire. In James Abernathy's eyes, London was the only civilized corner of the world, and he couldn't see why the sheikh insisted on living outside its environs. He realized that El Kabbar was a fine horseman and possessed one of the most famous stables in the Middle East. Still, there was Hyde Park in which to ride, and he was sure the facilities were more than adequate. This time, however, he was grateful for the delay of the drive before the coming interview.

Even over the phone he had been able to tell that the sheikh was not pleased at the news Abernathy had received in the morning's mail. Abernathy had thought El Kabbar would be relieved that the blasted girl had surfaced at last. After all, they had been searching for her for over six years. Reigning sheikhs were notoriously arrogant and Philip El Kabbar was more difficult than most. However, as his agent, Abernathy was extremely well paid to put up with that arrogance. There wasn't any question that he'd continue to do so, not in today's economy.

When Abernathy entered the library El Kabbar didn't look any more pleased than he'd sounded on the phone. His black brows were knit in a frown over stormy blue-green eyes. "Where is it?" he asked curtly.

"I have it here." Abernathy strode briskly forward and placed the package on the Sheraton desk. "I opened it, as I do everything addressed to you." He paused before adding apologetically,

"I had no idea it was anything of a personal nature." He started to turn away. "Now, if you don't need me..."

"Sit down and quit trying to escape, Abernathy." El Kabbar was crossing the room with swift strides, his tall, lean body as lithe as a cat's. From his clothes it was evident he had been about to go riding when he'd received the phone call. Abernathy fervently wished the sheikh had continued with the plan. Perhaps he would have expended a little of his anger on his horse.

Abernathy repressed a sigh as he obediently sat down in the wing chair beside the desk. "Of course, Sheikh El Kabbar. I'm only too happy to be of service to you. I merely didn't wish to intrude."

"I doubt that I'm going to be overcome with emotion," El Kabbar said cynically. He flicked on the desk lamp before removing the plain brown paper from the package with impatient hands. "Unless that emotion is anger. You could say I'm a trifle annoyed with our little runaway."

"Not very little any longer, judging by the photograph on the cover of that magazine," Abernathy said mildly. "You must remember that she's no longer the child of fifteen she was when she disappeared."

"Must I?" El Kabbar asked as he opened the jeweler's box. The sheikh's face was impassive when he looked down at the medallion, but his hand suddenly tightened, snapping the box shut. He picked up the copy of *Rolling Stone* and glanced at the picture. "A rock star. I should have known Pandora would pick a profession suited to her rather bizarre mentality."

"She's turned into quite a raving beauty, hasn't she?" Abernathy permitted himself a small smile. "Who would have thought such a little tomboy could be transformed into the woman in that picture?" He had only seen the girl once, when he had picked her up at the airport some six years before. The next day she had decided to run away. She had left only a sealed note for Philip El Kabbar and a great deal of turmoil behind her. That girl had been thin and wiry, with silver-blond hair that had been brutally chopped into a boy's cut. From the photograph it was clear all that had changed. Pandora

Madchen's features were by far the most classically beautiful Abernathy had ever seen, and her great dark eyes were truly magnificent. In the white satin Grecian toga that bared one shoulder her slim body was everything a woman's form should be. Her bosom might even be considered a little too voluptuous for her small body. It wasn't likely any man would complain, however. Pandora emitted an aura of sensuality that almost reached out and touched, stroked... Abernathy shifted uncomfortably in his chair. It was a very disturbing quality. "Do you suppose that wild orange hair is dyed or a wig? Why would she try to cover her own hair? The color was quite lovely, as I remember."

Philip El Kabbar didn't look up from the magazine. "A wig. But it wouldn't surprise me if she's had her head shaved and is bald as a jaybird underneath the damn thing. There wasn't a note?"

Abernathy shook his head. "Just the magazine and the jeweler's box."

The sheikh picked up the magazine and crossed to stand in front of the fireplace. "I suppose you've read the article?"

Abernathy shrugged. "Most of it. A good deal of it concerns the artistic merits of the group itself. Evidently Pandora and Nemesis are very well thought of by popular musicians."

"Nemesis?" Philip's gaze lifted swiftly.

"That's the name of the group itself. Rather fanciful, isn't it? I wonder if she thought of it herself."

"Probably." Philip looked down into the heart of the crackling fire. "Give me the bare bones of the story. I can do without the critical review."

"No one appears to know her last name in the United States. She's known only as Pandora. Evidently that's the thing to do in rock circles. It adds a certain mystique." His lips pursed disapprovingly. "Most exasperating. Your detectives might have found her if she'd used her surname. She's been in the public eye for almost two years."

"That long?"

Abernathy nodded. "The group had a hit single about that time and became very popular. The men in the group are all British, so it's probable that she linked up with them here in London."

"Then why didn't the fools find her? No city is that large."

"It's understandable. They were looking in the wrong places." Abernathy's expression was faintly reproachful. "You gave us no hint that she was interested in music. You said she had ambitions as an equestrienne."

"I also said that you couldn't put her into any cozy pigeonhole, blast it. There aren't any limits where she's concerned. She doesn't even know they exist." His hand clenched around the magazine. "Why the hell didn't they listen to me?"

"I'm sure they were thorough. Blackwell's is an extremely efficient agency." Abernathy could see that he wasn't getting through and sought for an out. Unfortunately, he had been the one to hire the detective agency when the Madchen girl ran away. "Have you phoned her father in Sedikhan and informed him that she's been located?"

El Kabbar nodded curtly. "Right after you called me. He wasn't at the dispensary so I left word with his assistant."

"Undoubtedly he'll be overjoyed when he hears the good news."

"Undoubtedly," El Kabbar said caustically. "He lost a horse-crazy fifteen-year-old and finds an orange-haired twenty-one-year-old rock star. He'll be over the moon."

"She's still his daughter," Abernathy offered quietly.

There was a short silence.

"Yes, she's still his daughter," El Kabbar finally said. "Whatever that means. Madchen never treated her with anything but complete indifference. When I told him she was missing his reaction was a philosophic shrug. No, you can't say they were exactly close."

"Is that why she ran away? I thought she was just rebelling at being sent away from Sedikhan to school here in England."

"No, there was more to it than that." El Kabbar's lips were suddenly a tight line. "Nothing is ever simple when it comes to Pandora."

"Isn't it?" There was a note of speculation in Abernathy's voice.

El Kabbar noticed it, and his lips curved in a cynical smile. "And, no, she wasn't my mistress, Abernathy. I've never indulged myself with teenage Lolitas. I like my bedmates with a degree of maturity and experience."

Abernathy was well aware of that. El Kabbar's latest affair had been with a beautiful opera singer who possessed both of those attributes. Still, he had wondered a bit at the sheikh's reaction when Pandora Madchen disappeared. El Kabbar had flown to London at once and supervised the search personally for almost a year. That, in itself, had been unusual. His demeanor during that period had been even more surprising. There had been moments when the man looked positively haggard. "I would never have intimated such a thing. I know that Dr. Madchen has been in your employ for a number of years. I'm sure you would have been just as concerned for the daughter of any—"

"The devil I would," El Kabbar bit out. "My employees are well taken care of, but I wouldn't go through that hell as part of any fringe-benefit program."

"Then why—" Abernathy broke off. He was coming dangerously close to exhibiting a curiosity that he knew would not be welcomed. He had learned long ago that one ventured past the sheikh's wall of reserve only at his own express invitation. "She appeared to be an unusually appealing child. A little quiet, but very polite."

"It must have been one of her better days," El Kabbar said dryly. "Pandora was seldom quiet and never polite. She was wild as a hawk." His lips twisted. "From the looks of this photograph I'd say she hasn't changed all that much."

"You have to admit she's made a success of herself, in a rather offbeat manner."

"She could never have done it any other way. She hears a different drummer." El Kabbar turned away from the fireplace and strode briskly toward the desk. He dropped down into the massive leather executive chair and tossed the magazine carelessly on the blotter in front of him. "Does Blackwell's have a branch in the States?"

"I believe so," Abernathy said cautiously. "If not, I'm sure they can make arrangements with a suitable counterpart." He frowned. "But why? We already know where Miss Madchen is located. Since she used a return address it's obvious she wanted us to know her present whereabouts. It's not likely she'll disappear again."

"Pandora never does what's likely. I have no intention of losing her again." He met Abernathy's eyes steadily. "Besides, at last I have some work that your very thorough detectives can sink their teeth into. Not only are they going to keep Pandora under surveillance, but they are going to protect her as well. Who knows what kind of weird element she's surrounded herself with?" For an instant there was a flicker of humor in his eyes. "Though I doubt if anything could be worse than the tiger she was cuddling before she left Sedikhan."

"Tiger?" Abernathy asked in bewilderment.

El Kabbar made an impatient motion with his hand. "Never mind, it's a long story. Just see that she's protected. I also want a complete dossier drawn up on her, down to the brand of toothpaste she's using at present."

"How soon do you want it?"

"Tomorrow afternoon." He ignored the other man's stifled exclamation. "Did you say she's playing in San Francisco day after tomorrow?"

"According to the list of concert dates in the magazine. It's the last concert on the tour."

"I have some loose ends to tie up here, but I should be able to get away by tomorrow morning. Have your man report to me at the Fairmont tomorrow afternoon at five."

"They might not be able to complete a dossier that quickly."

"They'll do it," El Kabbar said grimly. "They've been milking me for the last six years—it's time they produced. I'm extremely displeased with them."

Abernathy swallowed nervously and stood up. "I must get back to the office and make a few telephone calls. Do you have any further instructions?"

"That's all." Then, as Abernathy started for the door, he added, "No, wait. Find a way of contacting Mrs. Zilah Seifert. I believe she and Daniel are cruising in the Caribbean on their yacht *Windsong*."

He smiled sardonically. "Let her know the lost lamb has been found. She has a peculiar fondness for this particular lamb."

Abernathy nodded briskly. "I'll see to it. If there are any problems, I'll phone you in San Francisco. Good day, Sheikh El Kabbar." He strode hurriedly toward the door. This time he was allowed to leave and he closed the door behind him with a sigh of relief.

It was foolish to be nervous around the man after so many years in his service, but the sheikh could be a very intimidating man. Abernathy wouldn't like to be in the detective's shoes if he didn't come through with that dossier on schedule. For that matter, he wouldn't want to be in Pandora Madchen's place either. The sheikh's emotions were exceptionally strong and volatile where she was concerned. Personally, he found it much more comfortable to be ignored by the man except when needed.

Philip leaned back in the chair, his eyes going compulsively to the magazine he'd thrown so carelessly on the desk. Lord, she was beautiful now.

Even in that grotesque wig she shimmered with allure. But then, he had known she would be beautiful eventually because as a child she had possessed an enchanting grace and loveliness. Strange that he hadn't noticed it more often when she had tagged around after him like an eager little puppy. He supposed he'd always been vaguely conscious of that glowing promise, but it had been all but obscured by her fire and intensity. He wondered cynically if that intensity was still as strong. Perhaps she had found, like most beautiful women, that society requires nothing more of her than a tempting body and an accommodating nature.

For some reason that thought sent a surge of rage through him, and he reached impulsively for the jeweler's box on the far side of the desk. He flipped it open and stared down at the medallion, trying to subdue his anger.

He had given her the medallion to safeguard her when she was a child running wild around the village and encountering danger at every turn. Everyone recognized the rose and sword as the insignia of his house, and it had placed her automatically under his protection and possession. She had accepted the fact that she belonged to him. She knew he didn't give up what was his. Not ever. Yet she had returned the medallion without even the courtesy of a note. What the devil did she mean by that gesture?

His eyes narrowed thoughtfully as he reached out to touch the gold of the rose. With the Pandora he had known six years ago, he would have been able to guess. Sometimes he had felt so close to her, he could almost read her thoughts. Now he couldn't be sure. Beauty had a way of corrupting anything it touched, and Pandora had lived with the knowledge of her own exceptional beauty for years now. Perhaps she had changed.

If that was the case, her sending the medallion could mean any number of things. Invitation, rejection, reconciliation.

Of course she had changed. Everyone changed with time and experience. And the Pandora who was smiling out of the picture with such smoldering sensuality had obviously gained a lot of experience along the way.

Well, he'd find out how those changes would affect him very soon. Because, even if she didn't realize it, she still belonged to him. He had only to decide in what capacity.

TWO

THE RECTANGULAR JEWELER'S box was lying on her vanity table when she walked into her dressing room after rehearsal the next evening.

Pandora recognized it at once, and for a moment the breath stopped in her lungs. So soon? Philip never hesitated once a decision was made. She had known he'd react at once—she'd even counted on it. Still she was stunned. She walked slowly across the room and flipped open the lid of the box, already knowing what she'd find there. There was a small card lying on top of the medallion. Her hands were shaking as she picked it up and read the bold script.

"It's not that easy. There's a car waiting in the alley outside the stage door. Don't keep me waiting."

No signature. There was no need for one. Both the tone and the handwriting itself were poignantly familiar. *It's not that easy.* She would have laughed aloud if she hadn't been afraid she would burst into tears. There was nothing easy about this situation. She had never been so frightened in her life. Yet beneath that fear was an exuberant joy that was growing with every second. She was going to see him. Dear, sweet heaven, after six years without him she was going to *see* him again!

She closed her eyes and drew a deep breath. She mustn't get so excited. She had to convince Philip she was as sophisticated and blasé as the other women he took to his bed.

She'd be fine in another moment. She had learned to disguise her feelings in the past two years. She would be able to fool Philip if the masquerade didn't last too long. She would have to accomplish her purpose quickly.

She opened her eyes. Her reflection in the lighted vanity mirror was not reassuring. Her dark eyes were enormous in her white face. What if Philip didn't think she was even pretty? Other people seemed to, but beauty was a matter of taste. She felt panic rise in her. What if—No, she wouldn't let herself have these doubts. Move. Philip was waiting. The game was about to start. She wished she hadn't thought of that. She had always been too impatient to be any good at games. Philip was the one who excelled at them.

She unpinned her wig, threw it on the vanity, and took off the nylon wig cap. Her hair tumbled about her shoulders in a silver cloud. That was better. She must concentrate on being alluring and block out all those doubts. She turned and strode hurriedly toward the tiny adjoining bathroom.

Thirty minutes later she stood before the mirror again, gazing at herself critically. The makeup was just right, enough to accentuate her features and give her an air of sophistication, but not enough to look cheap. The square neckline of the black velvet gown she was wearing was so low that it barely covered the tips of the breasts swelling from its soft folds. Too sexy? It was a little obvious, but there was no way it could be too sexy for what she had in mind. She turned away from the mirror before any more doubts could weaken her resolve and walked quickly from the dressing room.

In a short time she was standing before the door of Philip's suite at the Fairmont. The door swung open at her first knock. He was dressed in white slacks and a collarless shirt in a forest green shade that turned his eyes to deep turquoise. He was just the same: the high cheekbones, the sensual mouth, the tanned hardness of his lean, tough physique. The air of leashed power that surrounded him was the same as well. She felt a curl of excitement in the pit of her stomach and had to stifle the impulse to walk into his arms and nestle there. Home. She was home again.

"That orange monstrosity is a wig, thank God. Abernathy was wondering if you'd dyed your hair," Philip said tersely. "At least you look civilized." His glance touched on her creamy breasts. "If not precisely modest."

"Am I allowed to come in, or would you like me to stand out here so that you can continue tearing my appearance to shreds?" Her voice was light and mocking. She only hoped her expression was equally composed. "Hello, Philip. It's good to see you again."

"Come in." He turned away. He was angry. Six years ago that fact would have devastated her and it disturbed her even now. "And while you're at it you can dispense with the polite chitchat. If you were so happy to see me, it wouldn't have taken you six years to renew our acquaintance."

"There were reasons." She followed him into the room and closed the door. She laid her black evening bag on the low chest to the left of the door and smiled sweetly at him. "Isn't it enough that I'm here now? I may have been a little slow, but I did contact you eventually."

"No, it's not enough." He crossed the room and dropped into the cane chair by the window. "And what the devil did you mean by sending me the

medallion? I don't take back that particular em-
blem. You know that. It's not just a pretty piece of
jewelry."

She nodded serenely. "Yes, I know. That's the
reason I returned it. We both know it's a symbol of
possession. I found I didn't like the idea of being
owned." She shook her head reprovingly. "Really,
Philip, the system you have in Sedikhan is feudal. I
wonder that I didn't object before to wearing it like
a meek little vassal."

"The vassalage system evolved because it was
beneficial to both parties. It provided service to one
and protection to the other." His lips tightened
grimly. "I don't recall that you objected to being under my protection when it suited you."

"But that was because I was a child." She smiled
again. "I understand the barter system much better now."

His eyes narrowed. "Was that supposed to be
loaded with implications? Don't try to be subtle,
Pandora. You never were able to pull it off." There
was a quick leap of anger in his eyes. "You never
used to want to play word games."

"I never was capable of it. There's a difference."

He studied her for a long moment. "You've changed," he said slowly.

"I've grown up. We all do eventually."

"Let's find out just how much you've changed." He held out his hand. "Come here and let me look at you."

She felt her heart give a little jerk. She only hoped her reaction hadn't shown in her face. She moved forward, swaying with deliberate grace. She felt a little shock as she slipped her hand into his. "I hope you think I've improved," she said lightly. "That little scarecrow had a long way to go."

"Oh, I don't know," he drawled. "I had a certain fondness for that scarecrow." He pulled downward with sudden force, and she found herself on her knees before his chair, looking up at him with startled eyes. His gaze was suddenly on the lush cleavage revealed by the low neck of her gown. "Though I can see a couple of advantages to the new you."

She wouldn't blush. "I'm glad. I suppose old habits are hard to break." She met his eyes. "I still want to please you."

His thumb began tracing a lazy pattern on the sensitive flesh of her inner wrist. "That's not an old habit, that's a new development. I don't recall your ever caring whether I was pleased or not."

Her lashes lowered. "I cared." Oh Lord, how she'd cared.

There was a sudden note of anger in his voice. "Look at me, dammit. You remind me of a blasted Khadim."

She kept her eyes fixed on the middle button of his shirt. "But you like Khadims." Her tone was gently teasing. "I remember that very well. There was always one on the horizon or one disappearing into the sunset. From what I read in the newspapers, you still use their services or that of their Western counterparts. Some of them are very lovely. Am I as pretty as they?"

His thumb abruptly ceased its movement on her wrist. "Are you inviting comparisons?"

She didn't answer. Her throat was so tight she didn't think she *could* speak.

"I take it silence is assent?" His voice was no longer curt, but a silky drawl. "That puts a different light on our little meeting. Interesting. But then you were always that, Pandora." He released her wrist and leaned back in his chair. "Why don't you get up and go sit on that couch across the room? I think putting a distance between us would be a good idea at the moment. A proposition like that has a distinct physical effect on a man that tends to cloud his judgment. I believe we need to resolve a few points before we take up the issue you've raised."

"If you like." She stood and crossed the room. "Though I'd have thought you would be accustomed to this sort of thing." She sat down on the couch and gave him a brilliant smile. "It's not as if I'm asking for any kind of commitment from you. We're both adults and know what we want."

"Do we?" He smiled cynically. "I know what I want. I've known since you walked into the room, but I'm not sure I know what you want." He paused. "Are you going to tell me why you ran away six years ago?"

She shrugged. "I left a note."

His lips tightened. "A note that contained two sentences: 'Don't look for me. I'll come back only when I'm ready.' Very melodramatic. Didn't it occur to you that it was also a little inconsiderate?"

For a moment her control broke. "No more than it did to you when you sent me away," she said fiercely. "I told you I didn't want to go. You wouldn't listen to me. I told you—" She broke off. "But that's all in the past. It's not important now."

His lips curved in a curious smile. "For a moment there I thought it did matter to you," he said softly. "My mistake." He stretched his legs out before him with the deceptively lazy grace of a stalking cat. "So what have you been doing all these years?"

She glanced away. "Nothing much. I had a few jobs. I managed to survive."

"You don't intend to confide in me?" He clucked reprovingly. "And we're such old friends, Pandora."

"It's not very interesting. I wouldn't want to bore you."

"On the contrary, I'd be very interested." He waved his hand in a gesture of dismissal. "All right, let's move on to more recent history. Let's talk about Luis Estavas."

Her eyes widened. "Luis? But how—"

"Or perhaps you'd like to tell me about your weekend with that Texas millionaire, Ben Danford." His expression hardened. "Or your current live-in companion, Neal Sabine."

"You've had me investigated," she said, her eyes wide with incredulity.

"You're damn right I did," he said harshly. "You stole those six years from me. I had a right to know who you were spending them with."

"Stole!" She shook her head. "You're impossible. Those were my years, my life, not yours." She was so indignant that for a moment she didn't realize what a lucky break this was. Philip had done her work for her. She wouldn't have to drop any subtle hints about her shady past or dangle poor Neal in front of him. She was already established as a woman of the world thanks to Philip's possessiveness. She tried to hide her relief beneath a careless laugh. "My men friends have been delightfully amusing." She paused. "And quite protective. Life can be difficult for a woman on her own."

"Financially?" He lifted a brow. "I understood rock stars made exceptionally good money."

"They do while they last." She made a face. "And good musicians can have lasting and lucrative careers. Unfortunately, I seem to spend money as quickly as I make it." She touched the velvet of her gown. "I like pretty things, and I have no illusions about my talent. I have a good, strong pair of lungs, style, and a body that's appealing enough in the scanty costumes Neal dresses me in. I'll coast along another year or so, but in the end I'll be replaced by a new craze."

"Still, you're very watchable. I think I might like to see you perform."

She tried to hide the sudden alarm she was feeling. He mustn't do that. She revealed too much of herself when she was on stage. "You don't like rock, and I'm hardly good enough to change your mind. You'd be disappointed."

"You're very realistic."

"The life I've lived hasn't encouraged anything else. I've learned to look for certain"—she paused delicately—"rewards in my relationships." She gave him the smoldering look Neal had taught her for publicity photos. She did it very well by now.

"That's the real reason I sent you the medallion. I thought we might come to an arrangement. You've always been very generous to women who please you."

His face was impassive. "You know I don't indulge in permanent associations. You were streetwise even as a child, and I never tried to hide my relationships from you. I haven't changed."

She laughed. "Does that report from your detective agency indicate that I'm looking for commitment?" She shook her head. "Permanency doesn't have any appeal for me either. It just so happens I have a three-month break after the concert tomorrow night and I thought we might spend it together."

His face was watchful. "Let's be very clear, shall we? You're offering to become my mistress for the next three months, with no strings attached, in exchange for my"—his lips curved in a mirthless smile—"generosity?"

Her throat was dry. "Yes. Does the idea appeal to you?"

"Oh yes, it appeals to me. You're a very beautiful

woman, and I've always liked a businesslike approach in my Khadims."

Khadim. There was no special emphasis on the word, yet it cut like a knife. She held her smile in place with an effort. "I remember that. Then are we in agreement?"

"Perhaps." His expression was intent. "There's something about your very tempting offer that makes me vaguely uneasy."

"Uneasy?"

"Perhaps it's my pride smarting. Maybe I enjoy having a woman put up at least a pretense of desiring me before the negotiations start."

Pretense. Oh dear heaven, who wouldn't want him? Her problem was that she mustn't reveal how much she wanted him. "I don't think you'll find me lacking in emotion." Her voice was a little husky, but maybe he'd mistake it for sultriness. "I think you know I had something of a crush on you when I was a kid. It would have been hard to miss. I thought an affair might not only be amusing, it might serve to exorcise you."

"Exorcise?" he repeated. "You make me sound like a devil incarnate. If you're going to be a successful Khadim, you're going to have to learn to choose your words more carefully. I'm not sure I like to be thought of in those terms." His eyes narrowed. "But I admit the idea of being a fantasy figure is highly erotic to me." He rose lithely and strode across the room. Before she knew what was happening he had pulled her to her feet. His eyes were no longer cool, but burning brightly, and she felt her heart leap wildly. "Did you fantasize about me, Pandora?" he asked softly. "About how it would be when I made love to you?"

She couldn't breathe. She could scarcely get a word out. "Yes." She knew her eyes were revealing too much. She tried to shrug carelessly. "A few times, I suppose."

"I'm beginning to have a few fantasies myself." His strong, graceful hands were lightly cupping her shoulders, kneading the flesh through the black velvet. His eyes had dropped to the fullness of her breasts. "Do you know that when you shrug the way you did just now that the neckline dips just enough for me to get a glimpse of the pink of your nipples? Just a glimpse, and then it's gone. Much more arousing than going topless. Did you plan it that way?"

"No." Her voice was a whisper. She was glad his eyes were no longer on her face, for her cheeks were suddenly hot. "I didn't know."

"Whoever created that gown did. Its purpose is very clear. There's nothing more voluptuous than black velvet against smooth white skin." His voice was suddenly thick. "You have magnificent breasts. Your skin has an almost luminous quality." One hand slipped slowly from her shoulder to her throat. "It reminds me of the women in the Delacroix paintings." His finger reached the upper slope of her left breast. The touch was gossamer light, yet heat rippled through her. "But all paintings should have an appropriate frame."

She felt as if she were mesmerized. She knew her breasts were tautening, swelling beneath his eyes. "Frame?" she asked vaguely.

He chuckled. "Why not? They're obviously crying out for attention. You'll be out of that gown in a minute anyway." His other hand left her neck, and the velvet was swiftly pushed off her shoulders. Then her breasts were free of the velvet, the bodice now beneath them, lifting, offering them in the frame Philip had created. His face was heavy with sensuality as he looked at her. "Lord, that's beautiful. I think I'll have a black velvet halter made for you and have it sewn with pink diamonds." His face slowly lowered until his breath feathered her nipple. "Black velvet, diamond hardness." His tongue licked delicately, and an electric shock sent tremors through her entire body. "Against white velvet." He sipped at her nipple, and she felt the muscles of her stomach clench. "And pink soft-ness." He was sucking gently, tasting, nipping, his words muffled and hot against her breasts. His cheek felt hard and faintly rough as he rubbed it against her. "Would you like that? You could wear it when I take you to bed... You're so pretty like this."

She could scarcely comprehend what he was say-ing. She was on fire. Strangely weak, yet vibrantly alive and yearning. "If you like. Whatever you want."

He suddenly stiffened. His head lifted jerkily from her breasts as if he were unbearably tempted to remain. "How very accommodating." His voice was still thick with desire, but it held a bewildering hint of anger as well. "What a good little mistress you're going to make, Pandora. Perhaps the most passionate one I've ever enjoyed." He swiftly put her bodice in order and stepped away from her. "But could it be that the offer of diamonds has something to do with that passion?"

She reached a shaky hand up to brush the silver-blond hair away from her face. She mustn't let him see how much that remark hurt her. It was terribly hard to look coolly at him when her body was aching with suppressed hunger. "I always did like diamonds." She smiled with an effort. "And pink ones sound lovely. You appear to be a little upset. Have you changed your mind?"

His gaze was once more on her cleavage, as if he were unable to keep his eyes away. "Not upset. Uneasy. You have a very primitive effect on me. I think I could easily form a minor obsession where you're concerned." He looked directly at her. "I don't permit myself that sort of reaction to women."

"I know." She hadn't meant to say that. Surface. Keep it all on the surface. "I mean, it's obvious that you're only interested in a casual affair. Surely a minor obsession wouldn't be intolerable. You'll probably be bored to distraction with me in three months." She mustn't push. She turned away with another shrug. "However, it's your decision." She strolled slowly toward the door. "I wouldn't want you to feel at all uncomfortable with it." She picked up her black velvet evening bag from the low chest by the door. She opened it, pulled out the gold medallion, and dropped it on the chest. "But until you make up your mind I think you had better keep this."

"An ultimatum?" Philip asked, his expression once more alert and watchful. "Sexual possession or none at all?"

"I hadn't thought of it that way, but perhaps that

is what I meant." She opened the door. "Good night, Philip."

"Pandora."

She stopped and looked over her shoulder inquiringly.

"You haven't asked about your father," he said with a cruel smile. "Don't you want to know how overcome with joy he was when I called to tell him you'd been found?"

She felt the blood fade from her cheeks. She'd thought she had armored herself over the years, but trust Philip to find a weakness and strike with blinding swiftness. For a moment she felt as naked and vulnerable as she had when she was a child.

"No," she said shakily. "No, I don't want to know." She closed the door so swiftly she didn't hear the violence of the curse Philip uttered behind her.

He took an impulsive step forward and then stopped. His hands clenched into fists at his sides. He had hurt her. He had known that if there was even a vestige of the old Pandora left, his remark would hurt her, and he'd deliberately used it to test the sophisticated facade that had filled him with such anger and frustration. Why did the agonized look on her face make him feel slightly sick? He had never been particularly kind to women, yet in the past his actions had never filled him with such guilt. Since the moment she had walked through that door, he had felt that the Pandora he had known was somewhere just out of reach, beneath the smiling sophistication. There was something wrong, something out of kilter with this Pandora. The change was too radical.

He walked to the chest and picked up the medallion she had dropped so carelessly. Why was he questioning the metamorphosis that he had always known would come eventually? She was a desirable woman, and he would be a fool not to take advantage of the offer she had made. He could still taste the warm sweetness of her breasts on his tongue, and he felt a sudden thrust of desire in his loins at the memory. No, there was no question that he was going to take her up on that offer. He was tempted to follow her now to the hotel at the address the Blackwell's man had given him.

His hand tightened around the medallion as he remembered that she wasn't alone in that hotel room. According to the dossier, one Neal Sabine had recently moved in with her. With a start he realized he was actually shaking with rage. He took a deep breath and unclenched his hand. His palm throbbed slightly from the welt the raised design had left on his flesh. For a moment he had visualized that black velvet gown being slipped off her body by the faceless man in the report. He had seen her smile and stretch out on the bed, hold out her arms . . . He shook his head to clear it. The emotion he was feeling was too strong. If he continued this way, the obsession of which he'd been so wary would grow until he could no longer term it minor.

He didn't like not knowing everything there was to know about this new Pandora. The Blackwell report had been annoyingly scanty. Blackwell's man, Denbrook, had seemed to think that Pandora's romantic affairs were all that he was interested in.

He turned and walked slowly across the room to the phone on the table by the couch. He picked up the receiver and reached into the drawer for the business card Blackwell's man had given him. Martin Denbrook. He punched in the number rapidly.

"Denbrook? Philip El Kabbar. I've decided I want that in-depth report as soon as possible." He paused as he remembered Pandora's obvious reluctance for him to see her perform. "And I want a ticket for the Nemesis concert tomorrow night. Not too close to the stage." Denbrook started to protest, but he cut him off. "I want it. Get one for yourself too. There are scalpers at every sold-out concert. Get it for me." He hung up a few minutes later. He sat on the couch and stretched his legs out before him, his eyes fixed abstractedly on the door that Pandora had closed behind her such a short time before. His uneasiness persisted, but he knew that no matter what he discovered behind Pandora's alluring mask, his decision was already made.

The surge of primitive jealousy he'd felt when he'd imagined her with Neal Sabine was too strong to ignore. Whether she wore the medallion or not, she still belonged to him. This was the last night she would spend in her lover's arms. He should have kept her with him instead of letting her go to that bastard, dammit. He had an idea he was going to get very little sleep tonight.

Pandora in concert was electrifying. From the moment thousands of daisies rained down on the screaming fans until the moment she disappeared into the smoke and strobe lights at the end of the long, circular runway that led backstage, she was riveting.

She was dressed in the Grecian tunic that seemed to be her trademark. It was the color of old ivory, and so silky and flimsy that it revealed legs as beautifully symmetrical as her body was curvaceous. But after the first few minutes neither Philip nor the screaming fans were conscious of her sexuality except in a subliminal fashion. It was her energy that captivated them. Her energy, and an emotion so raw and basic that it touched a response in every person in the audience. She exploded with it and thrived and shimmered in the flames that explosion left behind.

"She's fantastic, isn't she?" Denbrook asked as the lights went on. "I feel as if I've been put through a wringer and hung out to dry." He shook his head. "You know, I even forgot how luscious she is after the first few minutes. No wonder the concert was sold out."

"Yes, she's fantastic." Philip's face was thoughtful.

Seeing Pandora tonight had been a revelation. The woman behind the cool, sophisticated mask. So much power. So much emotion. Why had she tried to hide that emotion? Well, it would be interesting to find out. The next three months were going to prove very stimulating if tonight's concert was anything to go by. He rose. "I'm going backstage. Phone the airport and have the plane fueled and ready. Then go wait in the car."

Denbrook got to his feet. His expression was disapproving. "Why don't I go with you, at least until you get backstage? It's not safe to carry that little trinket in your pocket in this kind of crowd."

"I'm quite safe at the moment." There was a flicker of humor in the smile that touched Philip's lips. "Pandora has hung them all out to dry too."

It took him fifteen minutes to negotiate the cordon of security men that surrounded the performers, and his temper was more than a little on edge by the time a message had been sent to Pandora and he had been granted permission to go backstage. Evidently the security measures he had ordered were completely unnecessary.

She was still dressed in the thigh-length tunic, but she'd already shed that awful orange wig when he entered the dressing room. She looked up from brushing her hair. The annoying mask of sophistication was back, and it irritated him even more now that he'd seen what lay behind it.

"You must be very tired. That was quite a performance you put on out there," he said as he closed the door.

"You were in the audience?" She went still, halting the brush in midmotion.

"I saw a little of it," he said carelessly. "I may even be forced to go out to the lobby and buy a Pandora sweatshirt. I was impressed."

"Don't joke." The brush resumed its stroking rhythm. "I told you I didn't have any voice to speak of."

"But your lungs are every bit as admirable as you boasted." He paused. "I'm not at all sure you're the flash in the pan you claim to be."

He could see her hand tense on the handle of the brush. "That's because you're not a rock devotee. It's here today, gone tomorrow."

"Is it?" His look was quizzical. "Then we must make sure you have a little something to fall back on." He strolled toward her, reaching into his pocket as he did so. "I brought your medallion back."

"Did you?"

"But you didn't bring the box, so I was forced to substitute one of my own." He set down the object in his hand on the vanity in front of her. "I think you'll like this one better."

The box was perhaps two inches square and was

the most fabulous piece of artistry she had ever beheld. It was composed entirely of large square-cut emeralds set between rows of sparkling diamonds. She stared in disbelief. "It's magnificent," she murmured. "It must be absolutely priceless."

"I bought it. Nothing that can be bought is priceless." He opened the box. "But I think you'll find it an adequate demonstration of my generosity."

"I believe *adequate* is a gross understatement," she said dazedly. "I take it you've made up your mind?"

"Yes." He took the medallion out of the box and fastened it around her throat. "On consideration, I found the idea of this particular kind of possession totally irresistible." His eyes met hers in the mirror as his hands slid beneath the low neckline of the tunic to cup her naked breasts. "You're very responsive," he noted with cool objectivity. "You like my hands on you, don't you?"

"Yes." Her heart was beating so hard, she had trouble breathing. "I do like it."

His hands moved over her breasts in a slow massage that was like tongues of flame on her flesh.

"That's fortunate. They're going to be on you a great deal in the next three months. I may find it impossible to keep them off you, in fact.

"I hope you don't have any plans that can't be changed. I'm taking you away tonight."

"Tonight!" Her eyes widened. Then she gasped as his thumb and forefinger closed on one burgeoning nipple and pinched just hard enough to send a liquid burning to the center of her being. She closed her eyes until the tremors had abated slightly. When she opened them they were still clouded with emotion. It was difficult to gather her thoughts. "We're leaving tonight? Where are we going?"

His eyes were narrowed and his face heavy with sensual pleasure as he watched her response in the mirror. "To Sedikhan. Where else? I have to meet with Alex Ben Raschid early next month about negotiating a new treaty." He was lazily plucking at her nipples, enjoying the dazed look of pleasure the action was bringing to her. His hands moved around to lift her breasts, and he studied the shape of the nipples pressed against the thin material of the tunic. "God, that's lovely." He leaned forward, his breath warm on her ear. "This excites you, doesn't it?" he whispered thickly. His eyes were on her reflection in the mirror. "Another frame for you, Pandora. Perhaps I'll radio from the plane and have the servants install a full-length mirror in my suite. I love to see you excited."

Everything he did excited her. Just being in the same room with him excited her. "I have to pack," she said.

"No." His teeth pulled gently at her earlobe. "I'll buy you anything you need. Is your passport in order?" She nodded, her eyes fixed on the image of his dark, sensual face in the mirror. "Good. I'll send Denbrook to your hotel to pick it up and have him meet us at the airport. I want to leave as soon as you're dressed. You know I've never been patient when I wanted something." His tongue touched the sensitive cord behind her ear and a shudder went through her. "And I want you very much, Pandora."

She knew that. She could feel it in the hard tension of his chest as it pressed against her back. "All right." She leaned her head back against him and closed her eyes. What difference did it make? He was taking her with him—that was all that mattered. "I'll come."

"I want to see you again." His voice was a hoarse mutter as his hands left her breasts and fumbled with the back of her tunic. "Does this thing have a zipper? All I could think of last night after you left was how pretty you were jutting out of that black velvet. How good you tasted." There was an edge of frustration in his tone. "How the devil do I get you out of this?"

"It doesn't have a zipper. It slips over my head," she said dreamily. He wanted her. After all the aching years, at last he wanted her.

"Then take it off, dammit. I want to see you."

Her eyes flicked open. "Here?" she asked.

"Anywhere." His eyes were hot and smoky. "I want you. At the moment I wouldn't care if we were out there on that stage in front of your thousands of fans."

She felt a melting in every bone of her body. She didn't think she would care either. "Philip, I'm not..." She was interrupted by a new voice.

"Pandora, will you fasten this damn..." The door had opened, and through a haze she saw Neal in elegant tuxedo pants and a white dress shirt. He stopped just inside the door when he saw Philip. "Oh, sorry. Did I interrupt something? I just wanted you to fasten these damn cuff links." He strolled forward. "Be a luv and do them up for me?" He held out his wrist to her.

"What?" She shook her head and the room came back into focus. Philip straightened behind her and his hands fell away from her shoulders. "Oh, yes, of course. Neal, this is Sheikh Philip El Kabbar. Neal Sabine." Neal nodded civilly at Philip. Her hands shook as she fastened the cuff link. "I don't know why you bother to wear them. You never manage to get them fastened."

"Elegance, luv. I like to see the expression of shock on the birds' faces when they see the campy rock star in all this sartorial glory." He held out the other wrist, and while she fastened the cuff link he said genially to Philip, "They're the very devil, aren't they? Are you coming to the promoters' big do tonight?"

"No." Philip's voice was so dangerously soft that Pandora stiffened, and her eyes flew to his face. "And neither is Pandora. Sorry to disappoint you. She's coming away with me tonight." He turned away and crossed the room. "I'll wait for you in the car, Pandora." The door snapped shut behind him.

"He's the one, isn't he?" Neal asked quietly. His blue eyes were fixed musingly on her face. He had never seen her look so glowingly alive, not even when she was on stage performing. "He's the man you wanted to impress with our cozy little setup." His lips twisted ruefully. "If I'd known he was so intimidating, I might have hesitated a moment or two. I wasn't sure if he was going to leave quietly or order me beheaded first."

"They don't behead people in Sedikhan anymore," she said with a shaky smile. "Yes, he's the one."

"You're leaving for good?"

"You won't have any trouble replacing me. You'll find someone else. Maybe she'll even have a decent voice."

His face was grave. "We'll miss you. You're sure you won't change your mind?"

"I told you when we started out that it was only temporary, that there'd come a time when I'd walk away from it. It's not my kind of life. It's not what I want."

He bent and kissed her on the cheek. "Then go for what you do want. I'll be rooting for you." He straightened. "I'll send Gene and Pauly in to say good-bye. We wouldn't want his royal munificence to get impatient, would we?" He stood there a moment, looking down at her. "I remember the first time you walked into that club in Soho where we were playing. You were only sixteen and you looked like a hungry chicken."

"I was hungry," she said. "And scared. God, I was scared."

"I'd never have known it. You were the most boldly alive person I'd ever met." His lips curved in a whimsical smile. "It's a wonder I didn't go completely bonkers over you. Isn't it lucky that I didn't?"

"Yes, very lucky," she said gently. "I refuse to give you too much credit, though. It was probably my froggy voice that turned you off."

"Maybe." His hand touched her hair. All the light in the room seemed to be gathered in that silvery-blond mass. "I always did have a sensitive ear." His hand dropped away. "Well, if things don't work out for you, come back to us. I can always wear earplugs if you offend my sensibilities too drastically. Good luck, luv."

"Good-bye, Neal," she said huskily. "And thank you. Thank you for everything."

His shoulders lifted in a shrug as he turned away. "You gave more than you got. You always do. Keep in touch."

She watched the door close behind him, her throat tight with tears. So many years. She hadn't realized how hard it would be to say good-bye and walk away. She'd had her mind so fixed on the goal at the end of the road, she hadn't realized what treasures she had acquired along the way. She stood up and pulled the ivory silk costume over her head.

If things didn't work out, Neal had said. The memory of those words sent a frisson of panic through her. Things had to work out. She couldn't bear it otherwise. Her whole life was wagered on this toss of the dice. Oh Lord, they had to work out.

THREE

"GOOD AFTERNOON, SHEIKH El Kabbar. Everything has been taken care of, just as you ordered," Raoul Coupier said as he met them at the front door. The words were as casual as if it had been only a few hours instead of six months since Philip had left Sedikhan. Raoul snapped his fingers and two white-uniformed young boys appeared to fetch the bags from the limousine. His thin, pale face was as impassive as usual as he turned to Pandora.

"May I say what a pleasure it is to have you with us again, Miss Madchen?" he asked politely.

"Thank you, Raoul," she murmured, trying to suppress a smile. It was difficult to believe that he could be sincere, considering all the uproar she had brought to his serene, well-ordered life in the past. She had taken a heathenish delight in playing the most outrageous pranks just to see if she could disturb the cool aplomb of Philip's personal servant. She had never succeeded. "It's good to be back."

"I took the liberty of ordering dinner in your suite tonight, Sheikh El Kabbar," Raoul said as he preceded them across the foyer and down the gleaming, mosaic-tiled hall. "You must be very weary after your trip, Miss Madchen. The time difference can throw your system a bit out of whack."

"I feel fine." It was good to have Raoul as a bulwark between them. He was ignoring Philip's grim and forbidding demeanor with the habit of years. "I'm not at all tired."

"You've forgotten what a powerhouse of energy Pandora can be, Raoul," Philip said caustically. He stopped at the door of his suite. "Time zones and jet trips of thousands of miles scarcely faze her at all."

"I haven't forgotten." A pained expression appeared on Raoul's face. "Miss Madchen was always exceptionally enthusiastic in all her...endeavors."

"However, we'll definitely have dinner in my suite. I find I'm not as resilient as our Pandora. I don't bounce back as quickly as the dynamic young rock stars she's accustomed to dealing with."

The barb in his last statement was obvious, but Pandora felt only a sense of relief. At least he was getting it out in the open. He had been in a foul mood since the moment Neal appeared in her dressing room. He'd practically ignored her for the entire trip, involving himself in a voluminous stack of paperwork from his many corporations. In a way it had been easier for her. She hadn't had to keep up her guard, to maintain that nerve-racking air of sophistication. "Oh, I don't know. You should see us after two weeks of one-night stands. We practically fall into bed every night."

"I imagine you do," Philip bit out as he opened the door. "Though I'd guess you're very fond of one-night stands as well. Your suite is next door. Please join me in forty-five minutes." The door swung shut behind him with a force that was not quite a slam.

Pandora made a face at the door. Yes, Philip was definitely upset and on his imperial high horse. "Do you think I've been insulted, Raoul?"

For a moment there was a flicker of humor in Raoul's brown eyes. "I wouldn't presume to say, Miss Madchen. However, Sheikh El Kabbar has always been talented in that direction, as we both know." He had moved to the carved door a few yards down the hall. "I believe you'll be comfortable here. When I received the phone call from the San Francisco airport I facilitated the acquisition of the wardrobe the sheikh said you would require." His eyes rested for a fleeting moment on her full bosom. "He said you had filled out a trifle. I hope the clothing fits."

"I'll manage," she said with a grin. "I'm not any more of a clotheshorse now than I was in the old days. If you remembered boots and jeans, I'll be happy."

"Oh yes, I remembered those." He smiled faintly. "You were always at the stable or on the back of one of the sheikh's horses. It would be difficult to forget." He opened the door for her and stepped back, inclining his head in a small bow. "If there's anything I can do, please let me know. Again, welcome home, Miss Madchen."

"Thank you." Her throat felt a little tight. This *was* home. Far more than the large house on the other side of the village that she had occupied with her father. "It's wonderful to be home."

She closed the door behind her and leaned against it for a moment. She was here at last. She felt relief sweep through her. It was over. Her glance swept around the room, taking in the canopy bed with the ivory silk hangings, the white fretted windows, and the rich amber and wine oriental carpet on the floor. Her eyes were drawn to the door to the right of the bed. She knew it led to Philip's suite. She was very familiar with this room. It was the one allotted to all of Philip's Khadims. She remembered that once she had crept in here, filled with resentment and burning jealousy, to examine the place where the chosen ones were quartered. The beautiful ones who occupied his bed and received his passion. It had hurt so much, yet the temptation had been irresistible. It still hurt, she found. She mustn't think about the past. She was the one occupying this room now.

She walked quickly to the louvered closet and threw open the folding doors. Thank heaven for Raoul's good sense. There were not only sexy garments appropriate for one of Philip's mistresses, but sport clothes, and even a practical terry-cloth bathrobe. She took the robe from the hanger and strode swiftly toward the bathroom.

Thirty minutes later she had showered, shampooed, dried her hair, and was once more standing in front of the closet trying to decide what a worldly-wise woman would select to wear for an intimate dinner for two.

"The yellow silk." Philip's voice made her jump. She hadn't heard him enter. He was dressed in dark, fitted pants and a soft white shirt that clung to his broad shoulders and lean, hard waist. His dark hair was still damp from the shower and she was conscious of the familiar spicy scent of his cologne. "I told Raoul to get that particular dress for you. I like the texture of silk."

She could have guessed that. She had never known anyone for whom tactile sensations were as important. She had a fleeting memory of Philip's hand stroking Oedipus's mane, his long fingers strong, yet infinitely sensitive. "All right. It doesn't really matter."

"On the contrary, it matters very much." There was a glint of mischief in his eyes. "This one has a zipper. I heartily approve of zippers." The humor suddenly faded from his face. "I imagine Sabine did too."

"I have no idea." She reached for the yellow dress. "We never discussed it."

"You were too involved with experimentation to waste time on mere chitchat, no doubt," he said silkily.

Oh Lord, Philip was definitely on the attack. She had wanted to arouse his possessiveness, but not to this extent.

She shrugged. "I suppose so." She tried to smile

teasingly at him. It was very difficult with him glowering at her like an incensed raja. "You appear to be fond of demonstrations yourself."

"That's different," he said with royal disregard for logic. "You don't belong to him."

"And in three months I won't belong to you either," she said quietly. "This is strictly a temporary arrangement." She made a mocking obeisance. "As decreed by the most honorable Sheikh El Kabbar."

"We'll see when the three months are up," he said moodily. "I don't like giving up what belongs to me." He scowled. "And I didn't like you fastening his cuff links. It was too . . . intimate."

She blinked. "Fastening cuff links is intimate? Heaven forbid if I straighten a man's tie."

"You're taking my displeasure very lightly. In the past you weren't so unaffected by it."

She wasn't unaffected, but he mustn't know that. Philip held too many weapons already. "You're taking a small service far too seriously."

"I just wanted to clarify that your services, both small and large, belong to me," he said harshly. "I don't share."

"How selfish of you." She lowered her eyes demurely. "I'll try to remember."

"I'll be there to remind you if it slips your mind," he said softly. "Be sure of it, Pandora." He turned away. "I'll leave you to get dressed. I have some phone calls to make." He paused at the door. "Don't bother to wear anything beneath the dress. I do hate to waste time." He left the door open, and a minute later she heard the sound of his voice as he spoke on the bedroom extension. So intimate. As intimate as the last remark, which had taken her breath and frozen her to the spot with sudden shyness.

Please, not now. She was so close. She had to be bold and sure or everything would fall apart. She drew a deep, quivering breath and swiftly untied the belt of her robe.

Bold and sure. She mentally repeated the words like a litany through the almost silent candlelight dinner. Philip seemed withdrawn, even remote, as the white-clad servants brought the delicious dishes to the table that overlooked the fretted balcony. Was he still angry? She couldn't tell by his expressionless face. It was still twilight, and the candles on the table weren't really necessary, as the entire room was bathed with a golden light. It lent the room the luminous sepia tones of old photographs, giving the scene a strangely timeless air.

She never remembered what she ate and she knew she'd never remember the names or faces of the servants who attended them. The entire interlude seemed dreamlike, a vignette seen through a veil of antique gold. Then the table was being whisked away and Philip was handing her a crystal glass of wine as clear and golden as the twilight haze that surrounded them. The taste was golden, too, smooth and tingling on her tongue. "It's very good," she said as she stood up and moved to stand outside on the balcony. "Does it come from the south vineyards?"

"No, the north. They've been producing for over five years now." He followed and stood at her side, looking out at the lavender-shaded hills in the distance. "We started reclaiming some of the slopes of the hills that border the Madrona Desert three years ago."

There was an element of excitement beneath the

casual statement. Evidently the irrigation project was still as much an obsession of Philip's as when she'd left.

For as long as she could remember he had been endeavoring to turn this desert wasteland into fertile farmland. "I'd like to see it. I'll have to take a ride up into the hills and look at what's going on."

He frowned. "Not alone. There have been reports of bandit raids on the villages on the Said Ababa side of the hills. They probably have a camp somewhere in the highlands. That's one of the reasons I wanted to get back." His lips tightened grimly. "I think I'll just go on a little hunting party."

"I'll come with you." The words were impulsive, and she almost bit her tongue.

"The hell you will," he said curtly. "You have a more highly developed instinct for trouble than anyone I've ever run across. I doubt if that's changed over the years."

"Whatever you say." She lowered her lashes so he couldn't see the blaze of defiance she knew was there. "Perhaps I'll go to the vineyards instead."

His frown deepened. "As I remember, the last

time you went there you persuaded the workers to have a moonlight grape-stomping party. My overseer was foaming at the mouth."

"He wasn't very reasonable." Her lips curved with remembered laughter. "I was only trying to help. Everyone had a perfectly wonderful time."

"Such a wonderful time that they were too exhausted to show up for work the next day," he said dryly. "And you were just as bad off. I had to carry you home looking like something that had fallen into one of the wine vats."

She had rested in his arms, she recalled, with her ear pressed to his heart. He had cursed her softly and emphatically with every breath, but his arms had been gentle. It had been a lovely memory to hold close when there was nothing in the world but barren loneliness. "Dancing on the grapes is a tradition."

"Not half-ripe grapes," he said flatly. "And not when there's a very efficient press to do the job. You don't go within hailing distance of the vineyards until I have time to go with you."

She frowned mutinously. "I can't go to the hills. I can't go to the vineyards. Where can I go?"

"To bed, like a proper Khadim." His hands cupped her shoulders. "Where else?"

The words shocked her back to the present and her role. "Where else, indeed?" She took his wineglass and set it, together with her own, on the balcony balustrade. Her arms went around him. Bold. She had to be bold and desirable so that he would become too aroused to stop when he ... "Do you know that you've never kissed me?"

"Haven't I?" His hands were lightly massaging her shoulders through the yellow silk. "It seems as if we were beyond kisses before we even started." His eyes were suddenly twinkling. "But if you insist ..."

His lips touched hers. Delicate, sipping, sugar sweet and warm. So wonderfully warm. His tongue rimmed her lower lip, and she melted against him, opening her lips with a yearning that was as natural as that of the first woman. "I want you," she murmured. "Give me all of you."

She felt him grow rigid against her. Then his

tongue was plunging into her mouth in a joust that was hotly passionate and hungry. So hungry. She was almost breathless when he raised his head.

"You're going to get all of me," he said thickly. "Over"—his tongue entered her mouth again, weaving an erotic spell—"and over." His lips were buried in her hair now, and she felt his tongue enter her ear. "And over." She was trembling, and her knees were so weak she sagged against him. Did his other women react so passionately? Probably not. Perhaps he wouldn't notice, she thought in confusion. Shouldn't she be doing something? She drew back a little, her hands quickly undoing the buttons of his shirt.

"Pandora."

She looked up.

There was a tiny glimmer of amusement beneath the hunger in his face. "Don't you think we should go inside? I'm flattered that you should be so eager, but I really dislike performing in public."

She laughed shakily. "Well, it's more private than the auditorium in San Francisco." She turned and walked quickly from the balcony into the room.

"You didn't seem averse to performing there at the time."

He followed her into the room and closed the French doors. "I'm on my own home ground now." He took a step nearer so that he was directly behind her. With one sweeping motion, he slid down the zipper of her dress. "And I told you I won't share you."

His hands slipped inside the loosened dress. "Naked," he said hoarsely. "There was nothing in the world more erotic than knowing that you were naked beneath that flimsy layer of silk." His hands were squeezing her waist, his fingertips running over the supple muscles with a pleasure that was echoed in his voice. "While we were sitting there at the table I was thinking how beautiful you'd look when I took it off you." His hands moved slowly up her back, and with painstaking care he pushed the silk off her shoulders. "I don't know what we ate this evening." He pushed the bodice down another inch until it hovered over the tips of her breasts. "All I could taste were warm, sweet breasts." He drew the silk farther down until it fell about her hips. She felt dizzy. "And I wondered if the rest of you would taste as sweet." He suddenly jerked the material over her hips and let it fall into a pool at her feet, leaving her in only her high-heeled sandals. "Look as sweet."

Then the sandals also slipped from her feet as his hands encircled her waist and lifted her out of the dress. He held her for a moment, rubbing her against him with a raw sensuality that made her heart pound wildly. "And you do look sweet." He kissed her deeply. "And you taste..." He lifted his head, his eyes glazed with need. He drew a deep, shaky breath and slowly released her. "Not yet. I want to look at you for a few minutes. This golden half light was created for you." He took a few steps back, his eyes flicking over her with an intimacy that caused a tingling to start between her thighs. His hands finished unbuttoning his shirt and he stripped it off, his eyes never leaving her. "I don't want to make love to you in the dark. I want to do it now with you awash in this golden mist. I want to watch your silver hair flying around your face as I move in you."

She laughed shakily. "Then you'd better hurry. I don't know how long this light will last." She bit her lower lip. "I don't know how long I will, either. Do you want me to undress you?"

"I'll do it. It's faster." She watched him as he stripped with efficient swiftness. He had a beautiful body, she thought dreamily. Lean and tough, with tight, hard buttocks and a horseman's strong, muscular thighs. The cloud of dark hair on his chest looked soft and inviting to touch. "And that's the last hurried action we're taking tonight. Slow. Every move slow and easy." He was drawing her over to the wing chair by the French doors. "I want to play with you, get to know your body. I don't know how long I can stand it, but I want to try. Would you mind?"

"Not at all." She didn't know if he heard. Her assent had been a mere breath of sound. She was surprised the words came out at all.

"Good." He dropped into the chair and pulled her down on his lap, facing him. She gasped. The masculine hardness of his bones and sinews was a sensual shock against her softness. She had never felt so womanly before in her life. She was conscious of the pliant softness of each curve, the ripe fullness of her breasts, the slight swell of her buttocks against the hardness of his thighs. Good heavens, the differences between their bodies! He rubbed his chest lightly, teasingly, against her breasts, the soft mat of hair tickling the sensitive tips. She made a low sound deep in her throat and arched against him. "Philip."

"I know." He was undulating like a cat against her, his eyes closed with an expression of pleasure so sensual that it was an arousal in itself. "It's too much, isn't it? It's killing me too. I feel as if I'm going to explode any moment. Just a little more. Lord, you feel good against me." His eyes opened and they were clouded with a smoky intensity. His entire body was hardening against her, muscles taking on a tension that was unbearably exciting for her to feel. He kissed her temple. "Be very still. I want to pet you a little. It won't be long."

Then his hand was running over her with a skilled sensitivity that caused tremors to rack her with every deft stroke. His long, tanned fingers were lifting her breasts, rubbing the undersides with smooth gentle rhythm. She could feel the muscles of her stomach clench. The tension was rising within her until it was painful.

"So pretty." His hand moved down to her stomach. He laughed softly as he felt the tautness beneath his palm. "You're wanting me, aren't you? Do you know how wonderful that makes me feel? How much do you want me?" His fingers moved exploringly down between her thighs, and she gasped as they entered with one smooth stroke and began to move. She buried her head against his chest, her breathing coming in little pants. Unbelievable. It was unbelievable. "I think you want me quite a lot," he said thickly. His other palm was stroking the soft nest of curls, pulling, probing, tugging gently. "But not as much as I want you. It's a physical impossibility. I'm going to go up in smoke in another second. I've never wanted a woman like this before. It's tearing the guts out of me."

Even through the haze that was enveloping her she was conscious of the thread of anger beneath the hoarseness of his voice. Poor Philip, she thought vaguely. He always liked to be in control, but he was caught in the same sensual web that she was. Her lips moved lovingly on his shoulder. "It's all right, Philip. Everything will be fine."

He glanced down at her in surprise. Then, for a moment, there was an expression of exquisite gentleness that transformed the taut hardness of his face. "Yes, everything will be all right," he said huskily.

His arms shifted and tightened, and suddenly he was standing, carrying her toward the bed. He placed her on the cool, silk counterpane, and followed her down. His thighs were on either side of her. She could feel the thin dusting of hair against her own smoothness. Different. So beautifully different.

"Do you know what I'm seeing when I look at you?" he whispered. "Gold. Satin gold skin, silver gold hair." His fingers combed slowly through the thick length of her tresses before bringing two silky locks forward and winding them around her breasts so that only her nipples were revealed. "Just these lovely things are pink." He bent forward, his teeth pulling gently on one taut peak.

He was golden too. The light streaming through the French doors gave his bronzed skin a shining patina and played over the supple muscles of his shoulders. Her hands grasped those shoulders, and she arched up against him as she felt his tongue touching, his teeth nipping, pulling hot wires of sensation that led to every part of her body. "I want to memorize the taste of every sweet part of you. You should be savored." He closed his eyes. "But I'm too hungry. I'm starving to death, Pandora." His hands released her breasts and he was moving between her thighs. "And you are, too, aren't you?"

Hunger. Aching. Yearning to be filled. "Yes, I'm starving too."

He laughed huskily. "God, I love to hear you say that." He leaned forward to kiss her with such loving sweetness that joy welled and flowed, not easing the hunger, but blurring the edges with beauty.

He plunged forward. Pain! It lasted only for a moment, piercing, shocking her. But it was Philip who cried out and froze in her arms. No! He mustn't do that. "It's all right." Her hands released their hold on his shoulders and moved up to caress his cheeks. "Please. It's all right." It was better now, and she began to move, enticing him, reveling in him.

"The hell it is." His face above her was twisted with hunger as well as shock. "It's not all right." She moved again, and a shudder ran through him, "God, don't do that. I can't think."

"Don't think." She tried to tighten, to hold him closer. He made a guttural sound of need. "Just make love to me. I want you so much, Philip. This is *right*. Can't you feel how right it is?" Her voice was shaking with intensity. "Don't think, dammit!"

"Oh, God." His whisper was almost a prayer. "I *can't*. Not anymore." He flexed slowly, tentatively. Then he thrust forward and was lost. They were both lost in a rhythm so fiery it shimmered like flames. Golden flames in a golden room. Oh, love, Philip. Giving, taking. Flames rising, whirling in a vortex of tension and beauty. Exploding in an ecstasy that lasted forever.

Forever. Yet the room was still bathed in the

golden halo of twilight and Philip's hard cheek was resting against her shoulder. His chest was heaving with the harshness of his breathing, and his body was still shuddering with tremors. Her hand went up to stroke the crisp hair at his nape with loving fingers. He felt so much *hers* at this moment. So close. After all the years he had stood apart from her, just out of reach. Her own at last.

FOUR

"WHY?" HIS VOICE was low and intense. He lifted his head, and the harshness of his expression jarred her out of the dreamy euphoria she'd been experiencing. "Dammit, tell me why, Pandora."

"I love you," she said simply. "I always have. I always will."

There was a fleeting expression of shock on his face. "So you yielded your fair young body as some sort of sentimental offering?" He rolled away and got off the bed. He looked down at her. Her body was warm and glowing with loving, her lips soft and swollen. Something hot and wanting leaped into his eyes. His hands clenched into fists at his sides. "Cover up!" he said jerkily. "The party's over."

Yes, the party was over. She had known what his reaction would be, but foreknowledge didn't make his sudden rejection more bearable. She obediently pulled the satin sheet over herself.

He strode toward the bathroom, glancing over his shoulder with a menacing frown. "You didn't answer me."

"No, it wasn't a sentimental offering." Her eyes met his with clear honesty. "I tricked you."

His soft exclamation was followed by a violent curse as he disappeared into the bathroom and slammed the door. He was back in two minutes, wearing a pearl gray velour robe. He sat down beside her and gripped her shoulders firmly, anchoring her in place. "Talk," he grated through his teeth. "It just may stop me from strangling you."

"What do you want me to say?"

"You might start with Luis Estavas, my chaste little Pandora."

"He was with the Brazilian polo team," she said quietly. "Your detective should have looked into those weekend jaunts a little more closely."

"Horses," he said disgustedly. "I should have known it was horses. Danford?"

"A ranch in Texas." A tiny smile curved her lips.

"Horses, again." His lips tightened. "Sabine? Don't tell me, let me guess. When he's not a rock star he moonlights as a jockey?"

She shook her head. "He's a good friend and agreed to be part of the setup."

"Oh yes, the setup." The words were bit out. "Let's talk about the setup. How long has this plot been brewing in your tiny brain?"

"Since the day I ran away from your agent in London," she said. "I knew what I was going to do. I just didn't know how I was going to do it."

"But I'm sure it came to you soon. You're nothing if not innovative."

"It wasn't that easy." She smiled a little sadly. "I think the most difficult part was the waiting. There were so many years to get through before I could even think of beginning."

"Well, when you got around to it you made up for lost time." He glared down at her. "I don't like being lied to."

"I know that." She moistened her lips nervously. "But I couldn't think of any other way."

"Any other way than pretending to be one step above a whore? Well, let me congratulate you, Pandora. You played your role exceedingly well. You obviously have a flair for the vocation."

She flinched. "I did what I had to do. The only way I could be sure you'd take me to bed was if I was...experienced because that's the only type of women you let into your life." She shrugged. "I thought if I sounded like a gold digger it would make you feel safer."

"Safer?" His tone was incredulous.

She lifted her chin. "Safer," she repeated distinctly. "You're afraid of me, Philip. You always have been. You were so afraid of me that you had to send me away to England." Her lips twisted

Iris Johansen

bitterly. "You would have sent me to Timbuktu if you could have resolved it with your conscience."

"I sent you to England because you were fifteen years old and becoming a hoyden."

She shook her head. "You sent me there because you cared about me." She made a helpless little motion with her hand. "Oh, I don't mean romantically. I know what a scrawny mess I was then. But you did care for me." Her voice dropped to a whisper. "Maybe you even loved me. I think there's a good chance that you did. It was too strong, wasn't it? You wouldn't let yourself love any woman. You use them, but you won't let yourself love them."

His face was expressionless. "If you know that, then aren't you a bit of a fool to let yourself be used by such a ruthless womanizer?"

"Perhaps." Her eyes glistened with tears. "But I didn't have any choice. I love you."

"Stop saying that!" he said with soft violence. "You don't love me. You developed some sort of fixation on me when you were a child and never got over it. You always were the most obstinately single-minded person I've ever had the misfortune to know." He gestured to the bed. "And this was nothing but a pleasurable sexual episode."

"The hell it was!" She was up on her knees on the bed. "That wasn't 'pleasurable,' that was beautiful. Don't you dare call it anything else!"

"Ah! The real Pandora is finally emerging. How did you manage to suppress that wild streak beneath your Khadim disguise?"

"It wasn't easy," she said tersely. Her face was still stormy. "I knew I'd have to time it just right or give myself away. But that's not what we're talking about. What happened here was beautiful. Say it, Philip."

"It was beautiful," he said gently. "But that doesn't mean it was made in heaven. Sex isn't love, Pandora."

"I know the difference." she said. "I've always known it. It's you who's wearing the blinders." She drew a deep breath. "It's time you took them off. We've wasted too many years already. We're not getting any younger, Philip."

He had to smother a smile. She looked little more than a child draped to the shoulders in the satin sheet, with her enormous dark eyes so earnest. Where had his anger gone? A moment ago he had been furious. Why couldn't he ever hold on to that anger where Pandora was concerned? "Have you considered the possibility that it's you who's wearing the blinders?"

"No." She bit her lower lip. "I can't begin to have doubts now. I won't let myself. Everything would be empty if I did." She shook her head. "I know you too well to believe that."

"You don't know anything about me," he said roughly. He stood up and jammed his hands into the pockets of his velour robe. "Nothing. You've blown me up into some kind of fantasy figure."

"I know everything about you," she said clearly. "Everything. I've made a study of you since I was twelve years old, when you saved me from getting my throat slit in the bazaar. Would you like me to tell you what I know about you, Philip?"

"I'd be fascinated."

"You're self-indulgent, sensual, arrogant, and much too accustomed to getting your own way," she said calmly. "You're also highly intelligent, have a wonderful sense of humor, and are practically a workaholic when it comes to bettering the lot of the people here in Sedikhan."

His eyes narrowed. "Go on."

She moistened her lips. "You're a magnificent horseman and kind to animals. You won't permit yourself many friends, but you're intensely loyal to those you do have." Her lips twisted with pain. "However, you don't permit women to share your friendship. I think I was as close as you've gotten there." She paused. Oh dear, here goes. "Not that I can blame you. With a mother like Helena Lavade, it's amazing that you're as tolerant of women as you are."

He stiffened. "I don't believe I like being probed to that extent."

"You have a perfect right to resent it. Just as I had a right to resent that detective report you had drawn up on me. Only my excuse for prying was more valid. I knew I was going to have a battle on my hands, and I needed all the ammunition I could get."

"And what do you think you've found out about

my twisted psyche? Perhaps you should have turned your talents toward being a psychologist instead of a rock singer."

She ignored his sarcasm. She had known he would become defensive when she brought Helena Lavade into the conversation. "I found out you'd been hurt," she said quietly. "Your mother was an exceptionally beautiful woman as well as an extremely ambitious one. Helena was half-Sedikhan and half-English, and she was a Khadim. She wanted power and became your father's mistress. That was only the first step in her plan. Helena made sure that she became pregnant by your father. Then she demanded marriage as well as a great deal of money. She knew he wanted a son and she threatened abortion if he didn't give in to her demands." Pandora shook her head. "She should have known better. From what I've heard, your father was a great deal like you. He married her all right, but he refused to pay the blackmail, imprisoned her in her quarters, and had her watched like a hawk until you were born. She was furious and full of hate. She managed to escape a few weeks after you were born and took you with her. She was very clever, and the sheikh didn't find the two of you for almost eight years. Then he divorced Helena and brought you back to Sedikhan." She met his gaze. "I don't know what she did to you in those years, but the stories I heard in the bazaar weren't pretty. She couldn't punish your father so she punished you." Her hands suddenly clenched on the satin sheet. "I would have killed her," she said fiercely.

"Would you?" There was a curious tenderness in his face. "You always were a protective little thing." His expression hardened. "That was a long time ago. I have no need of either vengeance or sympathy now." He paused before adding deliberately, "And I have no need of you, Pandora."

She felt a swift jab of pain. "You do need me. You just haven't realized it yet. That's what this is all about." She lifted her chin. "I have to make you realize it."

"Well, you're not going to get the opportunity," he said curtly. "I'm sending you back to the United States tomorrow."

"No," she said with great certainty. "I'm not

Iris Johansen

going. I knew that would be your reaction, so I took precautions." She made a face. "Or rather, lack of precautions."

"I'd be interested to know how you think you can prevent me from sending you away. If you recall, I'm the reigning head of this province. I can do anything I damn well please with you."

"But you won't," she said. "Because I've borrowed a page from your mother's book. Not that I like the idea of being associated with that bitch in any way."

"Which page?" he asked, his expression suddenly wary.

"I told you the timing was very delicate," she said quietly. "Not only because I knew I couldn't keep up the pretense for long, but for physical reasons. I went to the doctor and had him chart my fertile period." She smiled shakily. "This is it. I could very well be pregnant with your child, Philip."

For the briefest instant he looked as if something had knocked the breath out of him. Then his expression was once more impassive. "Blackmail is an exceedingly ugly practice."

She sighed. "I was afraid you'd be suspicious. I can't really blame you. I have no intention of trying to force you to marry me. If you'll contact Abernathy in London, you'll find he's received a legal document absolving you of responsibility for any possible issue. If you like, I'll ask Neal if it's all right if I name him as the father. I don't think he'd mind."

"The hell you will." The words were so violent they shocked her. He was silent for a moment, fighting for control. "Your friend can father his own child. He's not claiming mine."

"No one's claiming your baby," she said soothingly. "There may not be a baby. I just wanted to make very sure there was the possibility of one. I know how possessive you are, and I know you'll keep me with you until you're sure one way or the other. That gives me a few weeks, maybe even more. I've never been regular."

"You're taking a big chance," he said quietly. "You could lose everything. There's every possibility you may end up with an illegitimate child. I have no intention of marrying you."

"I know you don't. I told you I didn't expect that. I just want to be with you. I want to be a part of your life. That will be enough for me." She smiled mistily. "Besides, even if you did decide to kick me out, I'd still have the baby. That would be wonderful. I've always been pretty much alone, you know."

Lord, how he knew that. He took an impulsive step forward. "Pandora..." He stopped. He stood there with disparate emotions fighting for supremacy within him: exasperation, amusement, and the poignant tenderness she had always been able to call forth so effortlessly. Then his expression clouded. "No. I won't be manipulated. If you want to play woman of the world, get some other man to pay for your favors."

"I do want to be your woman," she said softly. "And your friend. And the mother of your child. I want to be everything to you. And I don't want to sell, only to give, Philip."

He ran one hand distractedly through his hair. "Dammit, I'll hurt you. You know I'll hurt you. You *know* me."

"Maybe." She shrugged. "But if I am hurt, it may be worth it."

"Go away, Pandora." There was a note of pleading in the command. "For some reason I find the idea of hurting you distasteful."

"That's because you care about me. I find that very promising."

"Then on your head be it. I've warned you. As far as I'm concerned, you're no more than the Khadim I bought with that trinket in San Francisco. I'll use you when and where I please and ignore you at any other time. Don't expect anything else."

"I don't expect anything at all." Her eyes were enormous as she gazed wistfully at him. "I can only hope."

"*God!* What am I going to do with you?"

Love me. Only love me. "Knowing you, I imagine you'll do exactly what suits your fancy," she said lightly.

His lips tightened. "You're right. And we might as well start right now. After I've finished using a woman I prefer that she return to her own bed. I like to sleep alone."

"Of course," she said softly. "I'll leave at once."
She swung her feet to the floor, flinching a little as
she felt a tingle of soreness between her thighs.

Philip muttered a low, explicit curse beneath his
breath. "Oh, for heaven's sake, lie down again.
Tomorrow will do as well."

"You're sure?" she asked uncertainly. "I could..."

"Pandora," he said through set teeth. "Shut up."

"All right." She curled up contentedly in the big
bed again, happy with the reprieve. She hadn't
wanted to leave him so soon. "If you change your
mind, just tell me."

"Be sure of it," he said dryly. He untied the belt
of the velour robe and took it off. It was almost
dark in the room now, and he was only a sleek
shadow as he moved to the other side of the bed
and slipped beneath the sheet. "Go to sleep."

"I will." She was almost asleep already. The
physical and emotional release she'd experienced
was having an almost narcotic effect on her.
"Thank you for letting me stay," she murmured like
a polite little girl.

"It's only for tonight," he growled. "Don't make so much of it."

"Whatever you say," she said drowsily.

He lay there on his back, separated from her by the width of the large bed, yet imagining he could still feel her warm, yielding flesh. His own body was rigid as he brought up his arm to rest it beneath his head, his eyes staring straight ahead into the darkness. "Did I hurt you?" he asked jerkily.

"What?" She tried to struggle up out of the cocoon that was wrapping her in the silken fibers of sleep. "No, not very much."

"Well, I might have," he said harshly. "It would have been entirely your own fault, you realize. I'm not a gentle man, but I don't enjoy hurting women. If you'd had any sense, you would have told—" He broke off. His tirade was falling on deaf ears. He could tell by Pandora's deep, even breathing that she was asleep.

"Damn!" It was just like the maddening brat to drift peacefully off to sleep, leaving him in this aching void of frustration. He had just had her, but he was as hard and throbbing as when he'd held her on his lap in the chair and . . . He drew a long, shuddering breath and closed his eyes. He couldn't think about it. He had to think about how she'd tricked him, about the way she'd manipulated him as if he were a blasted puppet. He had always had control over his emotions. He would just have to practice that control now.

He was infinitely careful as he slid into her warmth. First she was empty and then she was full of his hardness. From the deepest reaches of sleep she was conscious of his gentleness as he began to move. How beautiful it was, she thought dreamily. Not like before, when it had been hard and fast and breathlessly exciting. This was slow and lazy and sweetly fulfilling. She tried to open her eyes. "Philip . . ."

"Shhh . . . I didn't mean to do this. I lay there half the night fighting it. But I can't help myself."

"S'all right." Her words were slightly slurred. "I like it."

He chuckled. "I'm glad one of us approves." He

bent down and lightly kissed one eyelid and then the other. The tempo of his thrusts escalated. She could hear the heaviness of his breathing above her and feel the tension building in him. She tried to help, but his hands were immediately at her hips, preventing her from moving. "No, I'm trying to hold on to what control I have left. I don't want to hurt you. I shouldn't be doing this again tonight."

"You should be doing whatever you want to do," she whispered. "I'll always want you, Philip."

He went still. "Will you?" He bent forward to kiss the delicate blue tracery of veins at her temple. "I think the only thing you want right now is to go back to sleep." With a flurry of powerful thrusts, he gained a fiery release from the tension that had tormented him for the past hours. Then he was gone, shifting off, but not away from her this time. He pulled her close, cradling her against his shoulder so that her hair fell on his chest in a silken silver veil. Gradually his breathing grew steady and his heartbeat slowed.

"Did I help?" she asked sleepily.

"I didn't mean to do that to you." His words

were stilted, his voice thick with disgust. "Pandora, I'm . . . sorry."

"Did it help?" she asked again.

"Yes. Oh, Lord, yes, it helped."

"Then that's all that's important." She gave his shoulder a drowsy kiss. "I like helping you. Good night, Philip."

He didn't answer for a moment, and when he did his voice was a little husky. "Good night, Pandora."

He wasn't sure she had heard him. She was asleep again.

He found it impossible to follow suit. He should have been pleasantly relaxed, but he found himself charged with a mysterious tension that had nothing to do with desire. Tenderness. Dear heaven, he had never felt such tenderness before. It was like an immense tidal wave sweeping through him. He didn't want to feel like this. Not about anyone or anything. He *wouldn't* feel like this. He liked his life the way it was.

Pandora would belong to him, but it would be in the way he chose. What that way would be, he hadn't the wildest idea at the moment. But one thing was certain: Making love to her again any time soon would be a mistake. He wanted her too much. That desire would give her a power he wasn't willing to yield to anyone. He would just have to stay away from her until that fever cooled. It shouldn't take long. No woman had ever managed to hold his interest for more than a few weeks.

However, it wasn't desire that was putting his every nerve on edge. It was the tenderness. That emotion was far more dangerous than sexual arousal. He would have to take great care to guard himself against Pandora and that bewildering gentleness she inspired in him. He wasn't aware that even as the resolve was made, his arm tightened around her in protection.

He was still holding her in his arms when she opened her eyes the next morning. The gray light of predawn was filtering through the windows, showing her his face, so close to her own. She lay there in blissful contentment for a little while, just letting the wonderful intimacy of the moment seep into her. How many times in the last six years had she daydreamed about Philip holding her like this?

He looked so tired. Dark shadows were painted beneath his eyes, and his cheeks were hollow. At the moment he looked every day of his thirty-eight years. When he was awake he was so filled with energy and strength that she had never been aware he could be as vulnerable as this. She felt a rush of tenderness that flowed into every part of her. She had loved him for so long, yet she had never felt this maternal protectiveness before. She dropped a light kiss on his cheekbone and reluctantly slid out of his embrace.

She tucked the sheet carefully around his shoulders and moved swiftly to the door. She mustn't push too hard. She had given Philip enough to digest.

It was probably her fault that he looked as if he had slept very little the night before. Poor Philip. He wouldn't like the disruption that she was about to make in his life. Well, that was just too bad. It was all for his own good, and it was up to her to prove it to him. But, for now, she'd back off and give him breathing room.

The sun was beginning to streak across the sky in a burst of pink and lavender as she crossed the stableyard. She paused for a minute to breathe in the fresh scents of earth and grass. She could feel the coolness of the breeze against her cheeks and the joy rising up in her. Dear God, how good it was to be alive on a morning like this!

She was about to turn and go into the stables when she heard a soft neigh. She glanced casually toward the fenced pasture and then froze. Oedipus! The black stallion gleaming in the first light of dawn had to be Oedipus. She was over the high fence in seconds and running along the edge of the pasture. He was so beautiful, with his clean, powerful lines and a wild pride that was evident in every muscle and tendon. She slowed to a walk as she approached him. She mustn't startle him. Oedipus had always been only half tamed, and he was easily spooked.

"Hello, boy! Have you missed me?" Her voice was a soothing murmur as she approached him. "I've missed you. It's been a long time, hasn't it? I've been around a lot of horses since I've been gone, but there's never been one like you." He was looking straight at her, but she couldn't tell if he remembered her or not. With Oedipus, she might never know. He certainly wasn't sloppy about revealing his affections, she thought ruefully. Everything about his nature was difficult and challenging. In that way he reminded her of Philip. Perhaps that was why she had always been so crazy about Oedipus.

"What are you doing out here all by yourself, instead of lazing in your nice warm stall?" She was next to him now and reaching out a careful hand to stroke his nose. It was velvet beneath her palm. He looked at her as if he understood every word she was saying. "But then, you never did like to be inside, did you? Neither do I. It's always better to be out in the open, running with the wind in your hair." She moved slowly to his side, her hand shifting from his muzzle to his mane. "What do you say we do that now, boy?" Then, using the fence as a mounting block, she was on his back, gripping strongly with her knees. As she expected, he put up a fuss, but it was only a token protest. After she had ridden it out he settled down beautifully. "You want it, too, you devil." She laughed softly. "You just wanted to give me a hard time. Now let's *go*."

She started out at an easy canter, graduated into a gallop, and then they ran flat out, circling the large pasture as if it were a racetrack. She bent low over his mane, talking, urging him on. Oedipus was silk and fire beneath her, and the wind was tearing at her hair with cool, careless fingers. It was glorious!

"Pandora!"

She flinched. Oh dear, Philip. She cast him a glance. He looked just as grim as he sounded. He was dressed in riding clothes, and his hair was slightly rumpled. That was unusual in a man as meticulously groomed as Philip and boded no good. He must have guessed what she was up to as soon as he had awakened and dashed down here to catch her in the act. Drat it, Philip always seemed to know when she was doing something that wouldn't meet with his approval. She slowed Oedipus and headed him toward the fence. "Good morning, Philip. Didn't Oedipus look beautiful? He runs like he's still a two-year-old."

"He's not two years old, he's eight," Philip said distinctly. "And he's learned a good deal of devilry in those eight years. For your information, the fact that he's out here and not in the barn does not indicate that the poor old nag has been put out to pasture. He has the unpleasant habit these days of trying to kick his stall down. Last year he tried to trample a stableboy." His eyes were blazing. "And you're riding him *bareback*!"

"He likes me," she said defiantly. "He's always liked me. He may be mean, but I know how to handle him." She looked Philip in the eyes. "He reminds me of you."

For a moment indignation and outrage conflicted on his face. "Why, you little scamp," he said softly. "I ought to—" He was suddenly chuckling and reaching up to help her off Oedipus's back. "I've never had a woman compare me to a horse before. Most particularly a nasty one."

"It's only at times that he reminds me of you," she amended. "Sometimes he can be quite lovable."

His hands tightened on her waist. "Brat. You've grown impudent over the years. You never would have had the nerve to insult me before."

"If I had, maybe your arrogance would have been deflated a little."

"I was never arrogant. I was merely always and inevitably right." He slapped Oedipus on the rump and the stallion cantered off. "Exactly as I am now."

"If Oedipus has become so violent, why do you keep him around?"

He didn't look at her as he took her elbow and began to propel her across the pasture. "A whim, perhaps." His lips twisted in a sardonic smile. "No doubt I feel a subliminal kinship for the devil." He frowned. "Regardless of the reason, you're to stay off him."

She didn't answer, but her face took on a mutinous look.

"Pandora," he said warningly.

"I can handle him," she burst out. "I understand him."

"The way you think you understand me?" He shook his head. "Don't count on it. All understanding is colored by one's point of view. Both Oedipus and I are capable of acts that you can't imagine."

"No, I don't believe—"

"Pandora, if I catch you on Oedipus again, I'll get rid of him."

"You can't mean that. Not after all these years. He belongs here."

"I mean it," he said flatly. "You've made sure that I can't send you away, but there's nothing stopping me from getting rid of Oedipus."

She gazed at him uncertainly. "You'd really do it?"

"Try me."

She looked away. "You know I won't do that," she said huskily. "I couldn't take the chance."

"Wise woman. I wish you'd be as reasonable about your own welfare."

"That's another matter entirely."

"And one you don't want to talk about," he finished dryly. "All right, my little ostrich, we'll drop it for the moment." He was silent until they had left the pasture and were crossing the stableyard. "That was a difficult stunt to pull off bareback," he said abruptly. "You obviously haven't lost any of your skill while you've been belting out rock songs to the panting populace."

"I rode every day," she said quietly. "The shows were only at night. That left all the daylight hours to do what I wanted to do. I'd ride for four hours in the morning and spend the afternoon working on college correspondence courses." She grimaced. "It nearly killed me to stay inside all that time when I wanted to be at the stables."

"Yet you did it anyway." He was gazing at her thoughtfully. "Why?"

She shrugged. "I figured it was better to be miserable than stupid. I told myself the mornings at the stable were my reward for that blasted studying. A fair exchange. Something I needed for something I wanted. When I finally got used to the schedule it wasn't so bad."

"And horses were what you wanted?"

"Always," she said simply. "I never wanted to do anything else. You know that."

"No glamour of the footlights for you?" His eyes searched her face.

She shook her head. "I never liked performing. It was all right once I learned to cope with it. It was better than being hungry."

His lips tightened. "You were hungry?"

"Of course." She looked at him in surprise. "I was fifteen years old with no job experience and just four pounds and a few pence in my purse when I ran away from Abernathy in London." She made a face. "The money lasted two weeks. I was lucky to stretch it that far."

"And then?"

"I managed," she said evasively. "You don't want to hear all that dreary business."

"Don't I?" he asked grimly. He was silent for a few minutes before he exclaimed violently, "What a fool you were! Anything could have happened to you."

"I was lucky," she said. "It wasn't all bad. I made

friends. That was important. It's easier to live with an empty stomach than with loneliness."

His throat felt tight. "I'm glad you found friends," he said. "Are you going to go back to your rock group?"

She felt a swift pang at the impersonal way he asked the question. She tossed her head and smiled. "I hope not. I hope I'm going to stay with you here in Sedikhan for the rest of my life." She tilted her head. "Do you suppose I could talk you into forming an Olympic equestrian team? I promise I'd bring home the gold."

"The United States has an excellent team. I know some people. I'll make a few phone calls." He paused. "I haven't changed my mind since last night."

"Neither have I," she said lightly. "I guess it's an impasse."

"Not for long." His smile was touched with grimness. "I'm going to make your stay here very unhappy, Pandora. You'll be glad to leave when the time comes."

"We'll see," she said blithely. "Are you going to the irrigation project this morning?"

He nodded. "As soon as I go back and shower and change. I didn't take time to do anything but throw on some clothes when I found you were gone. I knew you'd be looking for mischief somewhere, and the stable was the most likely place."

"I was just trying—" she started indignantly. She broke off. She didn't want to argue now. "May I go with you?"

"No," he said definitely. "You may not. You may go back to your quarters and paint your toenails or loll by the pool like any good Khadim."

She felt a quick, burning resentment. Philip evidently meant everything he had said about treating her like his mistress. "Oh well, I'll find something to do."

"That's what I'm afraid of. But whatever you do, be sure you're through doing it by dinner tonight. I plan on having a few guests and I want you to act as hostess." There was a touch of malice in the silky tone of his voice. "They'll be delighted to have such an illustrious personality at the foot of the table. Perhaps you should wear your orange wig."

"Perhaps I should. I threw it into my overnight case along with the other clothes I had in my dressing room. Are we expecting someone important whom I should try to impress?"

"It depends who you think is important." He paused. "I'm inviting the good Dr. Madchen."

Her stride faltered. "My father?"

"I thought it fitting that the two of you get together after such a long separation." He smiled faintly. "Don't you agree?"

She moistened her lips. "Yes. Yes, of course." It had to come sometime. She mustn't feel this wrenching pain. She should have known Philip would exploit any weakness he found in her defenses. "You were quite right to invite him."

They were crossing the courtyard, and Philip stopped her for a moment with a hand on her arm. "I can hurt you, Pandora," he said softly. "I don't want to do that. Give in, tell me you'll leave Sedikhan, and I'll cancel the dinner party."

She shook her head. "That would only be running

away." Her smile was bittersweet. "I haven't done that since I was fifteen. You didn't approve of it then, why should you now?"

"Pandora, dammit, I don't—" He broke off and drew a deep breath. "Oh, hell!" His hand dropped away from her arm, and he strode away from her and on up the stairs of the entrance. "Dinner is at eight." The heavy, studded front door slammed behind him.

FIVE

"I THOUGHT YOU were joking." Philip, dressed in impeccable black evening clothes, leaned indolently on the jamb of the door between his room and Pandora's. His eyes moved over her impassively. The thigh-length tunic she was wearing was of black velvet that clung to her body and left one shoulder bare in the Grecian fashion. Her lovely legs were encased in sheer black hose that flowed into high-heeled black sandals. The effect was blatantly sexual.

"I *was* joking." She smiled and touched the orange fuzz of the wig on her head. "But I thought it over and decided it would be appropriate for the occasion." Her dark eyes were burning in her pale face. "I've learned to give the audience what it wants."

"And you think your rather bizarre costume will do that?" he asked quietly.

"Well, it will give them what they expect, anyway." She lifted her head. "Will you be ashamed to sit opposite me at the dinner table?"

He straightened in the doorway. "No, I won't be ashamed." He walked toward her, his eyes searching her face. "But are you sure you don't want to change your mind?"

She shook her head so hard the orange curls danced like curling flames. "No," she said fiercely. "This is part of me, too, and I'm not ashamed either."

He offered his arm. "Then shall we go to the salon and greet our guests?"

She drew a deep, quivering breath and took his arm. "By all means."

Karl Madchen wasn't in the salon when they arrived, but the other guests were all present, and Raoul was quietly moving about the room, serving drinks. A small dinner party, Philip had said. She supposed it was small by his standards, but there were at least fifteen people in the room. The low murmur of conversation dwindled as they walked in the door, and Pandora was immediately conscious of the raised eyebrows and amusement her appearance was causing. She unconsciously stiffened and immediately felt Philip's hand tightening on her elbow. "Steady," he said in an undertone. "Orange wig or not, you're still the loveliest woman in the room. Remember that."

She experienced a little surge of warmth. "I'll do that."

"Then come meet your guests." His blue-green eyes were twinkling. "I can hardly wait to introduce you to the ambassador's wife. She always was a stuffy bitch."

If this dinner party was supposed to be a punishment, Philip was certainly going about it in a strange way. He introduced her to each person in the room. His hand was constantly beneath her elbow, and his manner was both regally possessive and fiercely protective. Only when he had made sure that she would have no problems did he allow himself to be drawn away by one of his business cohorts. Even then she was still conscious of his glance on her from time to time, and again it gave her that warm feeling of being treasured.

She was casually chatting with an eager young oil executive when she heard a familiar voice behind her. "Good evening, Pandora."

She went still. Karl Madchen had been born and raised in Munich and had never lost the trace of a German accent. She turned to face him. "Good evening, Father." She held out her hand politely. "How nice to see you again." He looked almost exactly the same. His short, powerful body was perhaps a little more rotund, his blond hair a little more silver than gold, but his eyes were still crystal gray, cold and remote as a high mountain peak. "You look very well."

His expression remained impassive as his gaze went over her. "You haven't changed."

She tried to smile. "I thought you'd say that. I have, you know." She raised her eyes to meet his in challenge. "Were you surprised when Philip told you I was here?"

He raised a glass of white wine to his lips. "Not at all. I always expected it. You've had your eye on him ever since we came to Sedikhan."

Not her eye, her heart. Her father had never understood that. "You don't object to your daughter becoming the sheikh's Khadim?"

"Why should I?" He shrugged. "You will do as you wish. It is your nature. As long as you do not interfere with my life, I'll have no quarrel with you."

She felt the freezing cold touch her. Why could he still hurt her like this? She tried to laugh. "I assure you that if Philip kicks me out I'll try not to do anything that might influence him against you." She took a sip of her champagne cocktail. "And I promise you that I won't come crying to you. I know how you value your comfortable lifestyle here in Sedikhan."

"I would appreciate that." He permitted himself

a small smile. "It would be foolish to pretend an attachment that never existed. Neither one of us ever needed anyone else. We were both very self-sufficient."

She lifted her chin. "No, I never needed you. I found that out a long time ago."

"You were always a bright child," he said objectively. "It was a shame you were so lacking in discipline."

Her hand tightened on her glass. "Yes, wasn't it?" Her lips felt numb as she smiled brightly. "I made your life quite uncomfortable. I'm sorry about that." She put her glass down on the rosewood table beside her with careful precision. "And now. if you'll excuse me, I think I see Philip signaling me."

"By all means don't keep him waiting." Madchen moved aside politely. "Perhaps we'll talk again."

She hoped not. How she hoped not! She was moving hurriedly across the room to Philip, conscious only of the need to escape. Philip's back was turned to her, and he didn't realize she was by his side until she slipped her arm into his. He broke off in the middle of a sentence to look down at her. His swift gaze took in her pale face and overbright eyes.

"All right?" he asked quietly.

Her smile was brilliant. "Of course I'm all right. I was just lonely."

His hand reached over to cover the hand that rested on his sleeve. "You're cold."

The whole world was cold. "My cocktail glass was frosted." She moistened her lips. "I'm fine. Really."

His lips tightened. "Perhaps we'd better go in to dinner."

"That would be a good idea," she said, smiling at Philip's bearded business associate with dazzling sweetness. "I'm starved, aren't you?"

During the meal she was conscious of Philip's eyes on her from the far end of the long table. She tried to make her earlier claim of hunger appear valid, but she was barely able to choke down a few bites. She gave up finally and concentrated on keeping up the appearance of gaiety instead. Smiling, chatting with the guests at her end of the table, she burned with a charm and vivacious energy that lit up the dining room. As long as she talked, she wouldn't be able to think.

It was the same in the library after dinner, as mint tea, coffee, and conversation ended the evening. She even managed to give a bright, meaningless smile to her father as she stood at the door with Philip, saying polite good nights to the guests.

Then it was over and everyone was gone. She turned away from the door, the smile still painted on her lips. "I think it went very well, don't you?"

"Oh, brilliantly," he said caustically. "Everyone was impressed. You were lighting up the dining room like neon. I should have had the lights turned off and saved on electricity."

"That wouldn't have been appropriate for a multimillionaire like you. You don't have to worry about coins for the electric meter." She smoothed the velvet dress over her hips. "Remind me to tell you how I jimmied the meter one freezing night in my flat in London. It might amuse you."

"I doubt it." He took her elbow and began propelling her down the long hall. "You haven't amused me so far tonight."

And the Desert Blooms

"I'm sorry. I'll try to do better next time. It's just as well your guests aren't as difficult to please. I think they found me sufficiently entertaining."

"You practically mesmerized them. I think they even forgot about that atrocious orange wig."

"On the contrary. The ambassador's wife asked me where I bought it. She said it was sure to start a new fashion." Her laugh tinkled like little silver bells. "Isn't that funny?"

"Hilarious," he said grimly. He opened the door to her suite, pushed her inside, and shut the door behind them. "The next social event in Sedikhan will probably see every woman sporting one of those monstrosities." His hands were swiftly removing the hairpins that held the wig in place. "Except you." He pulled the wig and cap off her head. Her hair tumbled down her back in a luminous silver stream. "I never want to see you in it again. Do you hear me?"

She lifted her brows in mock dismay. "You didn't like it? I'm truly crushed, Philip."

"You reminded me of Pagliacci," he muttered. He combed his fingers through her hair, loosening the confined strands. "A damned clown laughing to keep from crying."

She tensed. He was coming too close to the truth. She should have known he would. "I don't know what you mean."

"Stop that awful grinning." He whirled her around and unzipped her dress, shoving it off her shoulders and letting it fall to the floor. "Get out of the rest of those things while I find your night-gown."

He went to the bureau and riffled through the drawer. When he came back to where she was standing he was carrying a hyacinth blue silk night-gown. "This should do. The rest of that stuff seems about as substantial as cobwebs."

"As becomes a mistress's wardrobe," Pandora said. "Everything conforms to your standing order with the shop in Marasef, Philip. Blue predominating for blondes, scarlet for brunettes; yellow for—"

"Shut up!" He slipped the gown over her head and down over her hips. "I've had enough for one night."

So had she. "I'm sorry." She was smiling. He had

told her not to do that, hadn't he? She couldn't seem to stop. "You were looking forward to such a satisfying evening."

He picked her up and carried her to the bed. Was he going to make love to her? She hoped so. It might make her feel like a human being instead of a robot. He put her on the bed while he stripped back the spread and then tucked her beneath the satin sheet. It was cool against the bare skin of her back.

He was still standing by the bed, frowning down at her. What was he waiting for? "Hadn't you better get undressed?" He didn't answer. "Do you want me to help you?" She started to sit up. "You'll have to tell me what you like. I haven't had the benefit of experience, but I learn quickly."

"I don't think you do. I don't think you learn quickly at all. You just take any punishment that comes along and come back for more," he said hoarsely. His eyes were glittering strangely. "And no, I don't want you to help me undress so that I can use you as I did last night."

Use? What an ugly word for something as beautiful as Philip loving her. She wished she could tell him how wrong he was, but she could only gaze at him with that bright, meaningless smile.

"Damn!" He was tearing off his jacket and loosening his tie. Then he was in the bed beside her, drawing her into his arms. His hand was on the back of her head, burying her face in the crispness of his white dress shirt. His voice was shaking a little. "Stop it! Don't do this to me. Quit holding it in or we're both going to explode."

She couldn't let go. If she released the floodgates, she didn't know whether they could ever be closed again. "You don't want to make love to me?" she asked dully.

"No, I don't want to make love to you," he said harshly. "I want you to talk to me." His hand was stroking her hair with a gentleness that belied his tone. "I want you to talk about your father."

She stiffened. "I don't know why you want me to do that. It's not as if there's anything to say." There never had been. In all the years there had never been anything to say between the two of them. "I'm afraid there was no horrible scene or contretemps. That was what you expected, wasn't it?"

"I didn't know what to expect. I was using his presence as a weapon that I knew would hurt you, but I never expected this. Not this."

"You needn't worry. I'm not going to burst into tears and embarrass you." She laughed. It came out only slightly strained.

His hand hesitated and then continued its stroking. "What's it going to take to get through to you?" He was silent for a moment. "Would you like to know your father's reaction when I told him you were missing six years ago?"

"No!"

"Well, you're going to listen anyway. He didn't say one word. He just shrugged his shoulders. He exhibited the same concern as if I'd told him I'd misplaced a handkerchief."

"No, I don't want to hear any more." She tried to push him away, but his arms only tightened around her.

"Too bad. Because you're going to hear more. In the last six years I haven't heard him refer to you once. Does that hurt you, Pandora?"

"Why should it?" She was shaking and she couldn't seem to stop.

"It shouldn't, but it obviously does. It always will, until you face it. Karl Madchen has about as much emotion in him as a block of wood. He doesn't love you, Pandora, and there's nothing you can do to make him. It's not your fault, dammit."

The trembling racked her entire body. "Philip, please. Not now."

"Now," he said. "Do you think I'm enjoying this? I planned it all quite coolly. Inviting your father was to be the pièce de résistance, the crowning touch that would remove you from my life. I didn't know it would all go wrong." His voice was low and strained. "I didn't know it would hurt me too."

"Philip, I can't..." There was a loosening, a melting, deep inside her, and suddenly the tears were running down her cheeks. "It's the coldness I've never been able to bear. I've always known he didn't love me. I don't think he's capable of loving anyone." Her nervous hands were running restlessly up and down his chest. "I think marrying my mother was some kind of experiment for him. No wonder she divorced him. If she'd stayed with him, she probably would have frozen to death." She wiped her cheeks childishly on the crisp front of his shirt. "I'm sorry. I'm getting you all wet."

"I'll survive," he said gently. "Some people are born with something missing, Pandora. It's like being blind or crippled. It's not your fault that he doesn't have the capability of responding to affection."

"I think I know that now." Her words were muffled against his chest. "It took me a long time to work it out. There were always just the two of us, moving from place to place. I guess I was lonely. I couldn't understand why he wouldn't love me." Her voice was suddenly fierce with passion. "I loved him so much. It wouldn't have hurt him to love me just a little. I got so tired of being pushed away."

Philip felt a strange tightening in his chest. How incredibly painful that rejection must have been for the wild, passionate child Pandora had been.

"But I got over it." She laughed shakily. "I suppose you won't believe that after the way I fell apart so badly just now. It was the shock, I guess. He was very polite to me. He said it was silly to pretend an attachment that didn't exist, but that we could talk again." Her hand clenched on his shirtfront. "Perhaps I should ask him over for a spot of tea. He tells me that he doesn't mind my being your mistress as long as I don't come running to him when you tell me to hit the road."

Philip muttered a violent curse beneath his breath and his arms tightened around her. "How broadminded of him." He pushed her away, then his hands came up to frame her face as he looked down at her. "You really know how to pick the men in your life, don't you? You'd think that after growing up with an iceman like Madchen, you'd learn to discriminate between the people who are willing to give love and those who aren't."

"I didn't have any choice with you, Philip. It was just"—she made a helpless little motion with one hand—"there."

He closed his eyes. "Oh, dear God. I don't want this. I won't have it. You can't do this to me." He opened his eyes, and they contained the fierce rebellion of a caged hawk. "I'm not going to love you, Pandora. No matter how long you stay, you'll never be more to me than a body to warm my bed. Why don't you go away and save yourself a lot of grief? You're not meant to live like that."

"I can't go away," she whispered. Her eyes were glittering with unshed tears. "I have to try."

"And put us both through hell," he said flatly. "I hurt you tonight. I'll hurt you again. Give up."

"No," she said. She was almost numb with weariness. "There's no use your trying to talk me out of it, Philip. I'd like to go to sleep now, if you don't mind. I'm very tired." She had a sudden thought. "Unless you've changed your mind about wanting to make love to me?"

His lips twisted in a smile that held pain rather than humor. "Such a willing little Khadim." His hand brushed her cheek gently. "Go to sleep. I don't want you tonight." It was a lie. His body was as aroused and ready as it had been the night before. He was finding it impossible to be near her without such a reaction taking place. One finger traced the shadows beneath her eyes. "Maybe I'm getting old."

Her lips curved in a smile that caused his heart to jerk. "Oh no, not you, Philip." She turned her head and her lips were soft as they touched his palm. "Not you."

"Pandora..." He stopped. When he spoke again his words were halting. "It's not that you're not worthy of love. In spite of what you've experienced with your father, you mustn't think that. You have more value than any woman I've ever known. You have intelligence and drive and heart. It could be that I'm like your father. Perhaps there's something missing."

"I won't believe that." She nestled her cheek in his palm. "I want to tell you something. When I was a little girl I was always reading myths. I guess it was a natural interest, considering my name. I never liked the one about Pandora, but something about the tale of Persephone fascinated me. She was the daughter of Demeter, the earth mother, and was stolen by Pluto, the god of the underworld. Her mother refused to allow one grain of wheat to grow on earth until she was returned. Man would have perished from starvation if Zeus hadn't persuaded Pluto to let her go. They made a deal: Persephone was to spend three seasons on earth, during which time the earth would bloom and bear fruit. The other season she would return to Pluto in the underworld and the earth would be plunged into winter." Her gaze was pensive, far away. "I always felt a little sorry for Pluto. Perhaps all he wanted was his share of the blooming. I always hoped that Persephone brought it with her when she came to stay with him in the underworld. We all need our own time for blossoming." She kissed his palm again. "When I first met you, you reminded me a little of Pluto, imprisoned forever in a barren world. I've always wanted to bring you spring. I know how empty a winter world can be." Her voice was suddenly wistful. "I can do that, Philip. You're not like my father. Please, let me come in and try."

He was silent for a long moment. "Pandora, I *can't*." The words were torn from him. "Don't you see that?"

Iris Johansen

"No, I don't see that," she said with a weary sigh. She closed her eyes. "I think I'll sleep now."

Oh Lord, the stubbornness of her. He felt exasperation mixed with an aching tenderness wash over him. His hands pulled her head to rest on his shoulder. He kissed her lightly on the tip of her nose. "Yes, you go to sleep. Hostilities are definitely ended for tonight."

"I'm not hostile toward you." She didn't open her eyes. "I couldn't be. You're the only one who's fighting, Philip." She cuddled closer, and then stiffened. "I forgot. You don't like to sleep with anyone. It's all right to leave me. I'll be perfectly fine now."

"I'm sure you will." His arms tightened protectively around her. "I just don't happen to want to let you go at the moment." His lips touched her forehead. "Merely a whim, you understand. Pluto and I have been known to have them."

She laughed softly. "Yes, you have." She relaxed against him. "Well, whenever you want to leave, just go."

"I will," he promised. "Go to sleep."

She nestled deeper into his embrace. "Good night, Philip. I'll see you in the morning."

"Good night, Pandora."

He would get up soon and undress and put out the lights, but he knew he wouldn't leave her tonight. She was too vulnerable, in too much pain that he, himself, had inflicted. Strange, after all these years of living for himself, that he would want to soothe another's pain. Strange . . . and threatening.

Yet he knew, even if there was danger in it, that there was no question he was going to do it. But only because he wanted to. It was a whim, just as he had told her. Tomorrow, when they were both on an even keel, would be soon enough to lift his guard again.

S I X

RAOUL WAS WAITING for him in the stableyard. It was the fourth time in the last two weeks that the servant had felt compelled to meet him as soon as Philip rode in from the irrigation project. There was a worried expression on Raoul's face. Philip felt a sudden tension grip him and forced himself to relax. Pandora. It had to be Pandora, but it was probably nothing more than one of her usual brouhahas.

He swung down from the saddle and threw the

reins to the waiting groom. "Well?" he asked
tersely. "What now?"

"It's Miss Madchen," Raoul said hesitantly.

"I guessed that." Philip's tone was caustic as he
set off briskly for the house. "It's always Pandora.
What precisely has she done now?"

"She has a baby."

Philip stopped in midstride. "Would you mind
repeating that? Very slowly."

"She came back from the bazaar this morning
with an infant," Raoul said unhappily. "I'm afraid
the house is in something of a turmoil."

"She *bought* a baby at the bazaar?"

"No, I think she found it." Raoul's wide forehead creased in a frown. "At least I believe that's
what she said. Everything was very confusing at the
time."

Philip shook his head. Only Pandora was able to
bewilder his usually tranquil servant to this extent.
"There's more, isn't there?"

Raoul nodded reluctantly. "She also brought some
people with her. I gathered they have something to
do with the baby."

"People?"

"A snake charmer, two street musicians, a water vendor, and a young woman who is doing a great deal of caterwauling." His expression was pained. "She has a most distressingly shrill voice."

"Oh, my Lord. Why the hell did you let them all in?"

Raoul shrugged helplessly. "Miss Madchen was quite determined."

"Miss Madchen is always determined. That doesn't mean you can't say no."

"I seem to have problems there. She's very difficult to refuse when she wants something."

Philip couldn't argue with that. In the two weeks Pandora had been back in Sedikhan she had managed to turn his normally serene household upside down. She had been in so many scrapes, both in the bazaar and in the village, that he had been tempted to confine her to his compound. Obviously he should have done just that before this occurrence. A baby, for heaven's sake!

"I'm sure it was all done for the best of reasons,"

Raoul offered tentatively. "Miss Madchen is a very warmhearted young lady."

"That's generous of you," Philip said dryly. "Particularly since there's every chance you'll have to baby-sit this infant as you did that tiger cub six years ago."

"Oh dear, I hope not. I know very little about babies." He brightened. "Miss Madchen appears to be very attached to him. Perhaps she may want to take care of the child herself."

"That's what I'm afraid of," Philip muttered. He took the front stairs two steps at a time. "Where is she?"

"In the front salon," Raoul said. "There wasn't room in her suite."

Philip heard the music as soon as he entered the foyer. If you could call it music. There was some kind of stringed instrument fighting for dominance over the boom of a drum. Philip grimaced. "And you said the woman was shrill?"

"You haven't heard her yet," Raoul said gloomily.

Philip heard her a moment later, a loud wailing

that was enough to set his nerves on edge. "Damn, couldn't you shut her up?"

"Miss Madchen appeared to think it was a healthy outlet."

"She would." Philip was striding swiftly down the hall toward the salon. "Order the car ready, Raoul. We're about to clean house."

"Oh yes, sir. That would be splendid," Raoul said with heartfelt relief. "I'll see to it at once."

The sight that met Philip's eyes when he walked into the salon was enough to set his head spinning.

Two musicians dressed in brightly striped robes were sitting in the center of the Aubusson carpet, one playing a zither, the other a kettledrum. The wailing woman was huddled in a heap on the couch, her face covered with a portion of her brown robe. The scarlet-garbed water vendor, with his traditional girdle of copper cups and goatskin water bag, was arguing volubly with a young man in a white turban by the window. In the midst of the tempest, Pandora sat cross-legged on the floor by the musicians, calmly playing with a dark-haired baby of perhaps seven months.

"Pandora." Philip tried to keep his voice level. "Would you be so good as to tell me what is going on here?"

She looked up with an expression of relief. "Oh, Philip, I'm so glad you're home." She jumped to her feet, snatched up the baby, and hurried across the room. "They won't listen to me. I showed them the medallion, but I'm a woman and they don't seem to have the least respect for our sex. I don't really think Hanar likes the idea of the snakes, but they won't listen to her either, and she's afraid of her father-in-law." She stopped to catch her breath. "You run this damn country. Tell them they can't do it."

"Can't do what?" he asked blankly.

"Put a snake in his playpen," Pandora said impatiently. "I don't care if it is only a harmless little grass snake. It can't be sanitary." She shivered. "Besides, the whole idea is creepy." Her hand was rubbing the baby's back caressingly. "Imagine putting one of those things in with this darling."

"I don't want to imagine anything at all," he

said, trying to hold on to his patience. "I want to be told, very clearly and precisely."

"But I am telling you," she said indignantly. "They put a snake in the baby's playpen. There was actually one curled up on the mat sleeping in the sun when I first saw the baby by the booth at the bazaar, but I snatched it out and threw it away."

"It's obvious that we're going to have to play question and answer." He stabbed his finger at the weeping woman, who broke off in midwail, her eyes wide with apprehension. "Who's that?"

"Hanar, the baby's mother. She's really quite nice, if a trifle wishy-washy."

"The one who is afraid of her father-in-law and allows snakes to be put in the baby's playpen. Now, who is the father in question?"

Pandora pointed to the young man standing by the window being berated by the huge, bearded water vendor. "Beldar, the snake charmer, and that's his father, Damien, the water vendor."

Philip gestured to the musicians sitting on the floor, then gritted his teeth as the zither emitted a particularly shrill shriek. "Do they have to do that?"

"Well, I couldn't stop them. They're Beldar's brothers and absolutely crazy about the baby. It's the first boy born in the family. They think their music soothes the baby." She glanced down at the docile little boy in her arms. "You know, they may be right. Maybe he has a thing for heavy metal."

"Well, I do not," Philip said decisively. "Now that we have the cast of characters, let's have the scenario. You were at the bazaar this morning. You saw the snake in the baby's playpen and you took it out. What happened next?"

"Beldar came running up and tried to put it back in the playpen." Pandora's eyes were flashing with indignation. "I couldn't let him do that, could I? So I snatched up the baby and brought him here, until we could pound some sense into Beldar's head. He picked up the rest of the family as we went through the bazaar. I really think it's his father's fault. According to Hanar, he's very ambitious for his sons."

"Why does Beldar want the snake in the play-pen?" The absurd picture was at last becoming clear. Only a few more pieces to the puzzle and he would be able to restore order to this madhouse.

"His father told him he should do it to get the baby accustomed to reptiles. You see, Beldar's the success in the family, and his father wants the baby to follow in Beldar's footsteps." She lowered her voice. "Just between you and me, those musicians will never make it beyond the poverty level."

"I can see why. Their music has all the charm of a rusty nail being scraped across a blackboard."

"That's why Damien wants his grandson to go into the snake-charming business," Pandora said reasonably. "I can see that. Musicians have to be damn good to make it, while snake charmers don't have to—"

"Pandora," Philip interrupted. "Just tell me what I have to do to get these people out of my salon."

"It's very simple. Just do the voodoo you do so well. In short, intimidate the hell out of them. Make them promise not to put a snake back into the baby's playpen on pain of instant beheading or something."

"Is that all? Why didn't you say so?" He brushed

by her and strode into the center of the confusion. Pandora jiggled the baby on her hip as she watched Philip draw a royal cloak of arrogance about himself. No one could be more menacing than Philip when he set his mind to it. He moved from the musicians to the snake charmer to the water vendor to the weeping mother, speaking incisively and leaving no room for argument. Then he crossed back to Pandora and took the baby from her arms. "Stand aside," he said. "I hope we're going to have a parade."

She shifted to the side of the archway. He put the baby in the chastened mother's arms and returned to stand beside Pandora. He crossed his arms over his chest, his legs slightly astride. She had a sudden vision of Yul Brynner standing in that same pose in *The King and I* and had to smother a smile. All they needed was the "March of the Siamese Children," but thank heavens these musicians weren't going to supply it. They were scrambling to their feet and snatching up their instruments. The two men nodded nervously to her as they practically ran out of the room. Damien followed, scowling, his shoulders set and proud. The last to leave were Beldar with Hanar and the baby. The young mother gave her a tentative smile and scurried from the room.

"You did that very well." Pandora turned to Philip with a satisfied smile. "Of course, I'll have to go visit the booth periodically to make sure they don't backslide."

"No! I don't want you anywhere near that clan again."

"But I can't just let—"

He held up his hand. "I'll send a man down to check it out every other day," he said. "But you stay out of it."

"If you insist." Her expression was suddenly wistful. "I would like to see the baby again, though. Wasn't he sweet? Such big, dark eyes..." She broke off as her gaze fell on something across the room. "Oh, dear."

Philip frowned. "What's wrong now?"

"Beldar forgot something." She ran across the room and snatched up the small covered wicker basket on the floor by the window. "I hope I can catch him before he leaves." She hurried past him through the archway into the foyer.

"Pandora." Philip's voice was ominously quiet. "What is in that basket?"

She looked over her shoulder in surprise. "Beldar forgot his cobra." Her steps quickened. "I'll be right back."

Philip stared after her as she streaked out the front door in pursuit of the snake charmer. "Of course," he muttered dazedly. "Beldar forgot his cobra."

He was silent for a long moment, and then he began to chuckle. By the time Pandora returned he was leaning helplessly against the wall as he tried to suppress his laughter. "Did you catch up with him?" he asked, wiping his eyes.

She nodded. "I don't see what was so funny," she said crossly. "He was actually very rude to me. You'd think he'd be glad that I took the trouble to bring the cobra back to him. What's a snake charmer without a cobra?"

"What, indeed? Perhaps I ought to give him another lecture. Do you think that would help?"

"I doubt it. Anyone who would be dumb enough to put a sna—Philip, stop laughing. I went through a great deal of trouble and—"

His hand covered her lips. "And you caused a good deal of trouble today as well." His blue-green eyes were twinkling. "You're lucky that I can still laugh about it."

She kissed his palm affectionately, then took his hand away from her mouth. "I guess it was a little amusing," she conceded with a reluctant smile. "In retrospect."

"Definitely in retrospect." His palm tingled where her lips had rested. "Most of the humor you inspire seems to work that way. First horror and then amusement."

"You didn't seem to be any too terrified a few minutes ago. You play Lord-of-All-You-Survey with great dash."

"I've gotten a good deal of practice in the last two weeks." His lips twisted. "How did you manage to survive the past six years? You appear to live in the eye of a hurricane."

"I'm usually much busier than this." She paused

deliberately. "Painting my toenails and lolling by the pool makes me restless. Perhaps if you didn't leave me alone so much I wouldn't get into so much trouble. You could sort of keep an eye on me."

"Another setup, Pandora?"

"Not this time. However, I do get bored." Her eyes were glowing softly. "And lonely. I've hardly seen you since the night of the dinner party."

"I warned you that was the way it was going to be," he said impassively. "You should have expected it."

She nibbled at her lower lip. "You also told me that you were going to treat me as a Khadim," she said clearly. "You haven't been doing that." Her laugh was a little strained. "What good is a Khadim if you don't make love to her?"

"Perhaps I don't find this particular Khadim desirable," he said, not looking at her. "Perhaps one night was all I required."

"That's a lie," she said, her eyes flashing. "I know you want me. I can feel it. Why the hell don't you admit it?"

His gaze met hers. "All right," he said flatly. "I

want you. But there's no way in hell I'm going to take you. I'm not going to give you that advantage."

"Advantage? This isn't a tennis match or some kind of game. This is—" She broke off. She mustn't fall apart. It was just that time was passing so quickly and she was getting a little panicky. She might discover any day now that she was not, in fact, pregnant. Philip was no closer to accepting her now than when she'd arrived in Sedikhan. And, since the night of the dinner party, he seemed to have erected new and stronger barriers against her. "All right, you don't trust me. You obviously think I'm going to weave some sort of erotic spell over you once I've lured you into my bed." Her lips were trembling a little as she smiled at him. "I don't know why you think that, but I'll accept it. However, is there any reason why we can't spend just a little time together? We used to get along very well in the old days. I think you even enjoyed my company. If you don't want me to go with you to the irrigation project, there are still the evenings." She reached out an impulsive hand and laid it on his arm. "I promise I won't try to seduce you. No matter how much you deny it, I'm still a part of your life. I have a certain importance to you. If you won't accept me as a lover, perhaps we could be friends."

Her expression was so earnest when she told him she wouldn't try to seduce him, Philip thought ruefully. Didn't she realize that her hand on his arm was doing just that? Just a touch and his body was hardening, readying itself. "You said I didn't have women friends," he reminded her with a faint smile.

"I'd like to be the exception." Her hand tightened on his forearm. "Dammit, Philip, you know you're going to want me to stay in your life in some way or other. Why don't you admit it and behave sensibly? Maybe friendship is the way you can have me and your precious isolation too." Her voice softened. "And if not, then there's no harm done, and we'll still have had a pleasanter time than the last two weeks."

It was a mistake. Yet he knew he was going to make it. She was right. He was not going to be able to let her go entirely. She was too closely woven into the fabric of his life.

He reached out slowly and covered her hand with his own. "I've always known you were an exception to almost every rule," he said lightly. "Why not this one?"

The tension flowed out of her. "You mean it?" Her dark eyes were suddenly blazing with joy. "Oh, Philip, you won't be sorry. It will be beautiful, you'll see. We'll have such good times and do so many things together. We'll talk and ride and—"

He threw back his head and laughed. His eyes were warm and dancing as he looked down at her. She didn't think she'd ever seen them so warm. "So much for staying meekly out of my way until I have time for you in the evenings. I should have known it wouldn't last long."

She grinned back at him. Happiness was bubbling through every vein in a golden tide. "I'll be so good, you won't know me. I won't bother you at all and—"

His fingers covered her lips again. "I don't want a meek little Pandora prowling around, trying not to bother me." He grimaced. "Which is a good thing, considering that pose wouldn't last more than a day or two anyway." His expression was suddenly gentle. "Just be yourself."

"Okay. But in case you haven't noticed, I can be a little difficult on occasion."

"I can tolerate that. As I said, I've had a good deal of practice." His fingers dropped from her lips. "I believe I'm fairly easy to get along with." He frowned. "That was a most unladylike snort. It's quite true, you know. I have only one requirement for my friends."

"Really?" she asked warily. "And what's that?"

His stance was majestic, but his eyes held an elusive twinkle. "That they absolutely do *not* bring cobras into my salon."

Pandora slipped from the back of the chestnut horse and flipped the reins over his head. "Let's stop here for just a minute," she said over her shoulder as she ran to the edge of the cliff. She stood there, her eyes eagerly wandering over the scene below. "If you don't mind, that is," she added politely.

"Would it make any difference?" Philip drawled

as he swung off Oedipus and strolled over to join her at the edge of the precipice. "I've seen that look on your face before."

"Just for a little while." She dropped down on the ground and crossed her legs tailor fashion. "You've seen all this before, but it's the first time for me." Her gaze traveled eagerly over the carefully terraced slopes of green and brown that encircled the valley below. "It's beautiful, isn't it?"

"It's more than that," Philip said quietly. "It's productive and life-giving. When the oil is gone it will still be here furnishing grain and a livelihood for thousands of families. It took four long years, but we'll have a good harvest this fall." His expression was suddenly alight with eagerness. "Do you realize what a miracle is happening here? One pure, crystal drop of water and the desert blooms." His voice deepened with intensity. "It *blooms*, Pandora."

"I'm glad. You've worked very hard for that harvest." She felt a sudden rush of love for him. He cared so much, worked himself into exhaustion for the people in his province. How could he possibly think he was lacking in the capacity for emotion?

It was only in his personal life that he forbade warmth and caring. For the last two weeks she had been permitted past his defenses, and she had been filled with a delight that was close to euphoria. They had talked and listened to music. Taken long walks on the estate and in the bazaar. Ridden together, eaten together. She had even made the supreme sacrifice and had taken a stab at learning mah-jongg, a game that Philip was practically fanatical about. He had been surprisingly patient and, given a hundred years or so, she might even begin to like the damn game.

But none of it really mattered. All that mattered was the laughter and warmth between them. How wonderful it was to stand on equal footing with him at last. No longer a child or an enemy, but a woman he treated with surprising respect.

"What are you smiling about?" He sat down beside her, drawing up his knees and linking his arms loosely about them. His gaze of mock suspicion was fixed on her face. "I've learned through the years to be wary when you're particularly pleased about something."

"I was thinking that you're not nearly the chauvinist you pretend to be," she said lightly. "And that pleases me very much. I think you have more appreciation for women than you think."

"I have an appreciation for a certain few of your sex. I wouldn't want you to think I lack in discrimination. For instance, I find there are several aspects of your character that are admirably masculine."

"Masculine?" She repeated the word warily.

He nodded. "Determination, a sense of fair play, honesty. Given time, you might develop a good many others."

"Oh Lord, I spoke too soon." She covered her eyes with her hand. "Shades of Henry Higgins. But I'm no Eliza Doolittle, thank you. I think I brought myself up very well, and, if any further finishing is necessary, I'll do it myself too."

He snapped his fingers. "Independence. I knew I'd left out one of your laudable masculine virtues."

She shook her head. "Impossible," she murmured. "Utterly impossible."

His eyes were innocent as he said with deliberate

misunderstanding, "Not impossible. It's improbable a woman should have such qualities, but not—"

"Philip!" she said warningly, and then threw back her head and laughed helplessly. "I give up. You'll never change."

"How perceptive of you to realize that. My ideas and responses have been set far too long to change now. They will bend a little, perhaps, but they won't snap."

It was a warning. A flash of pain pierced through the happiness that surrounded her like a glowing cloud. No, she wouldn't let herself worry about tomorrow. Today was too beautiful to spoil. Philip did care for her. He had enjoyed these last days as much as she had. In the last week he hadn't even mentioned her leaving. Perhaps he was closer to a breakthrough than he imagined.

"I wouldn't admit that if I were you. A set mind is a closed mind." She smiled. "And a closed mind locks out all kinds of intriguing impossibilities that might become possible"—she paused—"someday."

He shook his head. "Fairy-tale thinking."

"Maybe." She suddenly rose to her feet in one

lithe motion. "And maybe not." She strode briskly toward the waiting horses. "I'm hungry, aren't you? I'm definitely ready for breakfast. I'll race you back."

He stood up and followed her at a more leisurely pace. "All this energy." He shook his head. "Where do you get it?"

She grinned at him as she mounted the chestnut. "I manufacture it at night. The elves have set up a magic spinning wheel in my room, and all night long I spin strands of energy to use the next day." The smile faded as she met his gaze. "But it happens only after midnight, when the rest of the world is asleep. You're invited to come in and watch. The elves won't mind." Her voice lowered to just above a whisper. "I won't either."

She saw his hand tighten on the saddle, and something flared hot and bright in his eyes.

Then his expression was once again veiled. He swung up into the saddle. "I don't think that would be such a good idea. Magic has a tendency to disappear when disbelievers appear on the scene. You'd better continue your spinning on your own."

She mustn't let the rejection hurt so much. She

knew he was wary of the effect she had on him physically. He had avoided touching her as if she were a plague victim. She could feel the tension in him whenever he brushed against her accidentally. She had thought, at first, that it was her imagination, that she was seeing her own desire reflected in him. But the signs were there, occurring too often to be mistaken. He wanted her. Why the devil wouldn't he give in and take her?

"Well, if you insist." She kicked the chestnut into a trot. "It's your loss. But you don't know what you're missing."

She was wrong. He knew exactly what he was missing, and that was the problem, he thought grimly. Perhaps this damnable abstinence would have been easier if he didn't know just how velvety her skin felt to the touch or how wonderfully tight she was around him as he moved . . . He felt the familiar heat begin to build in him and he checked the thought. He was having a difficult enough time resisting the emotional tumult of Pandora's nearness without risking a sexual maelstrom.

Pandora had reined in several yards away and

was looking back over her shoulder in puzzlement. "What's wrong?" Her face lit with a teasing grin. "Having trouble keeping up, Philip?"

He started to laugh. His eyes were suddenly dancing as he spurred after her down the road. "That's an entirely subjective matter," he said solemnly. "There are any number of ways of looking at it."

She frowned. "I don't know what you mean."

"Never mind. It's an in joke." He chuckled. "Or should I say, it's an up joke?" He had drawn abreast of her and was passing her in a cloud of dust. "What did you say about a race?"

The telephone call came when they were halfway through breakfast.

Pandora looked at Raoul in surprise. "For me? Who is it?"

"A Mr. Neal Sabine," Raoul said. "He's calling from Paris."

"Paris? What on earth is he doing in Paris?" she wondered aloud as she pushed back her chair. She was aware of Philip's sudden stiffening across the table from her.

"You're obviously going to jump up and run to find out," Philip said caustically. "You could call him back after breakfast."

"I'd die of curiosity before then. Besides, it might be important."

"What could be so important?" Philip's expression was forbidding. "You said you were through with Nemesis." His lips twisted. "Evidently that didn't include Sabine."

Oh heavens, Philip was going to be difficult. Why did this have to happen when everything was going so beautifully? Well, she'd just have to soothe him when she finished talking to Neal. She stood up. "Neal's my friend. He's done a good deal for me over the years. I'm never 'through' with friends," she said as she turned away. "I'll take the call in the library and be right back."

"Don't hurry." Philip took a sip of coffee, his expression hard. "We wouldn't want you to slight your 'friend' in any way."

She gave a helpless shrug. "I'll be right back," she

repeated as she strode swiftly out of the breakfast room.

She returned a little over fifteen minutes later. There was a worried frown on her face as she sat down opposite him. She took a sip of coffee. It was cold. She made a face and set the cup down in the saucer and pushed it away.

"Well?" Philip asked with a cool smile. "How is your old friend?"

"Not so good." She took a deep breath and said in a rush, "I have to fly to Paris today."

His face showed both shock and pain before he wiped it clean of expression. "Really?"

"Oh, for heaven's sake, Philip, don't freeze me out like this," she said impatiently. "I've *got* to go. Neal, Gene, and Pauly are in Paris trying to put together a European tour. They have a new lead singer." She smiled fleetingly. "Neal said she has a great voice, but my legs are better."

"If they have a new singer, why do they need you?" She was going away. She was leaving him just as— He blocked the thought out and ignored the wild explosion of pain that seared through him. He kept his features carefully expressionless as he tried to fortify himself against the corrosive agony he knew so well.

"Dubois, the promoter, is giving them problems. He doesn't want to invest heavily in an unknown." Her face was earnest. "It's important that everything about the tour be first-rate. It can be very traumatic careerwise for a group to lose its lead singer. A triumphant European tour would give them the clout to ask for big bucks when they return to the U.S." She paused. "Dubois always liked me. He handled our first tour after Nemesis was formed. Neal thinks I can persuade him to take a chance on the new girl too. It's worth a try."

"Is it?" He pushed back his chair and stood up. "Then, of course, you must go. I'll tell Raoul to have the plane readied while you pack."

She felt a little shiver of panic run through her at the impersonal way he was speaking. "I have to go, Philip. It isn't as if I want to run off to Paris. I'll fly in today, see Dubois tonight, and be back tomorrow evening at the latest."

He shook his head. "No."

She went still. "What do you mean?"

"Don't come back. I don't want you here." There was suppressed anger beneath the coldness of his words. "I don't want you in my life. I've told you that before."

Agony ripped through her. "You do want me. I know you do." Her chin lifted defiantly. "I'll be back tomorrow night and everything will be the same. You'll see."

His lips twisted. "Don't count on it. You know I seldom keep a woman for more than a month. Be sure to take that pretty trinket I gave you in San Francisco. There won't be any more forthcoming."

"You know I don't want your damn gifts," she whispered. "Why are you doing this to me?"

A shadow of pain passed over his face. Then it was gone. "Don't come back," he said again. "You'll regret it if you do."

"I'll be home tomorrow evening," she said huskily. "I'm not going to let you do this to us, Philip."

"This is my home, not yours," he said as he turned away. "You're an outsider here. Remember that, Pandora." He didn't look at her again as he strode out of the room.

She closed her eyes, trying to fight back the waves of pain. Why? She had expected anger, even jealousy, but not this cold rejection. It was as if she'd touched a trigger that had set off a hidden land mine. She couldn't believe that the laughing man who had sat beside her on the cliff this morning could have changed in such a short time. No. She wouldn't accept it. That warm, gentle man was still there beneath the hardness. She just had to find him again.

She opened her eyes and stood up. The sooner she got this Paris business over with, the sooner she could start that search.

Her steps were quick and firm as she hurried from the room to start her packing.

SEVEN

IT WAS ALREADY dark when the limousine pulled up in the courtyard the next evening. Philip's home resembled a gleaming palace from an Arabian nights storybook as the lights shone from the long, narrow windows and fell on the rich mosaic tiles of the courtyard. A palace that was remote and exotic and not at all welcoming.

Why had that thought occurred to her? Pandora wondered tiredly. She had always thought of the place as home, no matter how palatial and impressive it appeared to others. It must be because she was almost numb with exhaustion and so grimy that she bore no resemblance to the fairy-tale harem beauty who should occupy such an exotic palace.

She had wanted to change from these jeans and the tunic top before she saw Philip, but she had been too tired to bother. She'd had no sleep since she had left Sedikhan the morning before.

Dubois had been just as stubborn as Neal had suspected he would be, and they'd stayed up all night hashing out the tour details and getting the promoter to up the money. They had paused only for breakfast this morning, and the talks had continued until midafternoon. Dubois had been bull-headed, but he had acceded at last. Nonetheless, she had left for the airport feeling as if her nerves had been stretched on the rack. The scene that was waiting for her here would not help them any, she thought as she slowly climbed the steps. She had phoned from the airport in Paris to give her arrival time, and Raoul had rather sheepishly informed her that Philip was too busy to take the call.

It was Raoul himself who opened the front door

and came out on the steps. She gave him a rather strained smile. "Hello, Raoul. Have you been sent to guard the gates? I'm not sure I can put up enough of a fight to make it worth your while at the moment."

"Those were not my orders." Raoul's voice held a note of warm sympathy. "I was only told to tell the driver of the limousine to wait, and then to ask you to join the sheikh and his guest in the library."

"His guest?" Not her father. Please, anyone but him. She straightened her shoulders and lifted her chin. "All right, Raoul, I'll go straight in. I was going to change, but I wouldn't want to keep him waiting." Her lips curved in a sad smile. "That wouldn't be either polite or kind, would it? I'm sure he's eagerly anticipating this interview."

He took an impulsive half step forward. "Miss Madchen, perhaps it would be better if you went back to Paris for the time being. You can always return at some later time, when the sheikh is in a better frame of mind."

"That bad, is it?"

"I've never seen him quite like this. It would be

wiser for you to wait until his mood is a little less ..." He shrugged helplessly. "It would be better to wait."

She shook her head. "I won't cut and run. I knew it wouldn't be easy when I came back to Sedikhan." Her lips tightened with determination. "The driver of the limo can wait all night. I still won't be using him."

Raoul stood aside to let her pass, his expression still concerned. "I don't think ..."

"Don't worry, Raoul. I'll be all right. The library, did you say?" She walked quickly down the long hall. The door to the library was slightly ajar. She pushed it open and strolled into the room, unconsciously bracing herself for what she would find there.

It wasn't her father who was sitting in the chair facing the door. It was a woman. An extremely beautiful woman, with silky, dark hair and olive skin, ravishingly complemented by her scarlet chiffon gown. Her lips were parted in a warm smile as she gazed up at Philip, standing by the chair.

She must look like a tousled street urchin in

comparison, Pandora thought dully. "Hello, Philip," she said quietly. "I take it you have someone you want me to meet."

Philip was in dinner clothes, and looked as dark and dangerous as Oedipus at his most mettlesome. He turned to her with a smile that didn't quite reach his eyes. "Oh yes. I really thought the two of you should meet. Come here, Pandora."

She went forward to stand beside him. "That shop in Marasef is boringly predictable," she said huskily. "Brunettes do look good in colors other than scarlet. I think you'd look beautiful in a soft pink, Miss...?"

"Lenat," Philip supplied. "Natalie Lenat." His eyes were narrowed on Pandora's face. "You've guessed that she's your replacement, then?"

"How do you do, Miss Lenat?" Pandora said wearily. "I'm sorry you've been drawn into this. You don't deserve it."

"I don't understand," Natalie Lenat murmured in bewilderment.

"Send her away, Philip," Pandora said curtly.

"You're not going to discourage me by dangling another woman in front of my face."

"What makes you think she's here for your benefit?" Philip asked silkily. "Natalie and I are old acquaintances. We've enjoyed each other's ... company several times before."

"That's in the past," Pandora said jerkily. "Not now. Not in the future. I'm your future, Philip."

"No," he said very softly. "*You're* the past, Pandora. Accept it."

She was shaking. Each word was stabbing her like needle-thin icicles of pain. "Don't do this to me," she whispered. "You know you don't mean it."

"Don't I?" There was a reckless smile on his lips. "Your bags have been packed. Raoul has put them in the car by now. You'll have to forgive the haste, but Natalie needed the closet room, didn't you, sweet?"

There was a touch of sympathy in the brunette's face as she started to rise. "Perhaps I should leave you alone."

Philip's hand was immediately on her smooth,

bare shoulder, pushing her back into the chair. "No. Stay. I have a gift for you."

"A gift?"

"A very special gift." He took a step closer to Pandora, his hands sliding beneath her long silver hair. "Pandora won't need this any longer." He found the clasp of the medallion and released it, drawing the chain along her skin as he took the necklace off. It felt as if each link were cutting into her heart. "She's leaving Sedikhan."

"I can't take much more of this, Philip." She felt a fierce rage begin to smolder, burning away the pain like a mercifully cauterizing brand. "That's *my* medallion."

"Only as long as I chose to let you keep it," he drawled. "And I no longer choose to do that." He stepped behind the wing chair. "I wish to give it to my new Khadim." He put the medallion around Natalie Lenat's neck and held it there, without fastening the chain. "She has a lovely throat, hasn't she?"

"Damn you!" Pandora's dark eyes were blazing in her suddenly pale face. "Damn you to hell,

Philip. Who gave you the right to be so cruel to me? You didn't have to love me, but couldn't you have been kind at least?" Her voice was shaking. "What happened? Did you get scared again that you might give a little of yourself to someone else? Well, don't worry. I'm not sure that I want you to give me anything any longer. I might get frostbite. I think you like that winter world you live in." She stalked to the door, paused and turned. "And if I happen to have a child, I don't want him to live in that winter world either. That should relieve you. You can have your barren little planet all to yourself. We won't bother you again."

Then she was gone. Philip found himself staring at the door with blind eyes, feeling as if he were waking out of a nightmare dream into a nightmare reality. She had left him. It was what he wanted, wasn't it? Then why was he feeling this wrenching pain?

"You don't really want to give me this, do you?" Natalie asked softly. "It was only a way of hurting her?"

"Yes, it was only a way of hurting her," he said

dully. He slowly removed the medallion from around her neck with a feeling of intense self-disgust.

"I think you succeeded." She rose gracefully to her feet. "I believe you hurt her very much."

"So do I." He was suddenly nauseated as he remembered the look on Pandora's face. "I'm good at pulling wings off butterflies too."

"I think I should go pack." Natalie moved with lithe grace toward the door. "You do not want me here. It was all a game, as she said. Is that not so?"

"Yes," he said absently. He was still seeing Pandora's white face. "Of course you will be suitably rewarded for your time."

"Thank you. You've always been very generous." Her low voice was serene. "If you ever do really want me, you know I will come."

The door closed behind her.

He didn't want her. He didn't want any woman but Pandora. He would never want anyone but Pandora.

The knowledge struck him like a blow. Blind. My

God, how blind could a man be? Blind and frightened, just as she had accused him of being.

He felt as if he'd been in a fever since the moment she had said she was going to Paris. The pain had been so shockingly intense that he'd automatically withdrawn into himself, throwing up barriers with frantic urgency. Why hadn't he realized what he was doing?

There was a soft knock on the door and it opened a moment later. "Shall I tell the driver he may leave now?" Raoul asked with an aloofness that signaled extreme disapproval.

"The driver?" Philip looked up swiftly. "The limousine is still here? But Pandora . . ."

"Miss Madchen did not take the limousine," Raoul said. "She ran out the front door, but she didn't get in the car." He paused before adding accusingly, "I don't think she even saw it. She was most upset."

"I know that," Philip said. His lips were a thin line of pain. "Where did she go? Why the hell didn't you stop her?"

"I wasn't sure you would want me to. After all, you obviously desired her to leave."

"Where did she go?" Philip demanded. "I don't need you to turn the knife, Raoul. All I need to know is where Pandora went when she left here."

"She ran across the courtyard in the direction of the stables."

Philip muttered a low curse. He should have known she'd head for the haven of the stables. Then another thought occurred to him, and it stopped the breath in his chest.

"Oedipus," he breathed. "Oh, my God." He started for the door, fear a hard fist in his stomach. "Oedipus!"

She was running. The anger lasted only a few minutes after she left the library, and then the pain enveloped her in shimmering waves. She wasn't conscious of the tears streaming down her cheeks as she tore across the courtyard. She was only aware of the need to escape from that pain in any way possible. But there wasn't any escape. She knew that, even as she climbed the pasture fence and jumped to the ground on the other side.

Oedipus neighed softly. His dark coat shone in the moonlight with a silken luster. So beautiful. So powerful. So much like Philip, with his complexities and his remoteness. However, Oedipus wasn't remote tonight. He was warm and accessible as she threw her arms about his neck and buried her face in his mane.

"How about a run?" she said brokenly. "I need it. I want to outrun the wind tonight." Maybe she could outrun some of the pain as well. She slipped on Oedipus's back, and he stood like a statue until she nudged him forward. "Not the pasture tonight." She leaned far down and opened the gate, then urged him into a trot. "We need freedom, don't we?" In a few minutes she was away from the compound and on the road that led to the hills.

"Now." She was bent low over Oedipus's mane. "Run, boy!"

The wind was tearing at her hair as he stretched out at a blinding pace. She couldn't breathe, but for a little while she couldn't feel either as the scenery flashed by on either side of her. Oh Lord, how merciful it was not to feel. The moonlight shone on the road and she could see the hills looming dark in the distance.

The hills. She suddenly remembered sitting on the cliff overlooking those hills yesterday morning. Philip had been laughing and teasing her, his face lit with a rare warmth. She felt a bolt of pain rip through her. No, she couldn't go there now!

She tried to pull Oedipus in, but she had no reins. He was running faster now, covering the distance between the valley and the foothills with great speed. Then he was climbing, and she had to tighten her knees to keep from slipping off his sleek back. The cliff where they had stopped was much closer and she felt a sudden panic. She bent low, her arms encircling Oedipus's neck, pulling and trying to halt or break his stride.

The action only served to confuse him, and he suddenly reared, pawing the air. Her arms were torn from his neck and she felt herself slipping, falling . . .

She struck the hard, rocky ground with a jar that

knocked the breath out of her. For a moment she was only conscious of the struggle to get air. Then the pain in her lower back washed over her with an intensity that made her cry out. She was dully aware of a dampness between her thighs and a mist that surrounded her with ever increasing darkness.

She tried to lift her head and found she couldn't see any longer through the mist. How odd. It wasn't that dark tonight, she thought. Then the mists overwhelmed her, and she was no longer conscious of anything at all.

She was lying on something hard and unyielding, and the blanket that covered her was of rough wool. She heard Philip's voice fading in and out of the mists, but it was hoarse and rasping. She had never heard him sound like that before.

Yet when she forced her lids to open, it was undoubtedly Philip's face looking down into her own. His eyes were turquoise bright and glittering strangely. "My fault," she whispered.

He bent closer. "Don't try to talk. We have you

back in the first-aid room. You're going to be fine."
His hand, brushing a strand of hair from her temple, was trembling slightly. No, that must be her imagination. Philip was always rock firm and absolutely unflappable. But he was going to be angry. So angry. She must make him understand. "My fault," she murmured again. "Not Oedipus. I was stupid. It wasn't Oedipus."

A muscle in his jaw jerked. "No, it wasn't Oedipus's fault. I know that. Close your eyes and try to rest. Your father will be here soon, and we'll get you taken care of."

"My father?" She shivered suddenly. "Cold. I'm so cold, Philip."

"Hush, I know." His hand tightened on her own, as if trying to transmit his warmth to her. "It won't last long and then you'll never be cold again. I promise, Pandora."

Philip always kept his promises. She knew that. Yet even Philip couldn't perform miracles. How was he going to bring spring to a winter world? "My father doesn't know about spring." Her voice trailed away as her eyes closed again. "He doesn't know, Philip."

"Then we'll have to teach him," Philip said huskily. "I promised, Pandora. Just hold on for a little while longer and then I'll take over."

"All right, I'll try." Had he heard her? His hand was tightening on hers, as if he were trying to hold her back. Back from what? The darkness was warm and friendly and she was floating away on a gentle surf that cradled her like strong arms. Like Philip's arms carrying her back from the vineyard that night so long ago. Such a lovely memory...

"She's unconscious," Karl Madchen said from just behind Philip. His face was expressionless as he took a step forward and picked up her wrist. "Raoul said it was a fall from a horse in the hills. How long was she lying there before you found her?"

"Not more than two hours, perhaps less. I got together a party and rode after her as soon as Oedipus returned to the stable. We were very careful. We brought her down on that stretcher, but we reinforced it with special supports. I don't think there are any bones broken." He touched her jean-clad thigh gently. "However, she seems to be in shock and I think there's some bleeding."

"So I see. Well, we'll have to run a few tests. It may be nothing." Madchen was rapidly unzipping Pandora's jeans as he spoke. "I will let you know shortly. My assistant is waiting in the hall. Send her in, please. I will join you in the library when I have a report for you."

"I'm going to stay," Philip said hoarsely.

"As you like, but you'll be in the way. I can function more efficiently with you out of the room."

Philip muttered a curse and reluctantly released Pandora's hand. "All right. But hurry, dammit. I want to know right away."

"You will learn my diagnosis in good time. There are tests and perhaps X rays to be taken. I know my job, Sheikh El Kabbar."

Philip was aware of that. Madchen might be as emotionless as the Sphinx, but he was an exceedingly thorough, competent physician, or Philip never would have retained him all these years. "I want to know right away," he said again. "I'll be waiting."

He strode quickly from the room and proceeded directly to the library, pausing only to send Madchen's assistant into the first-aid room.

In the library he crossed to the cellarette and poured himself a stiff drink. Then he dropped into the large wing chair by the desk and stretched his booted legs out in front of him. He was filthy, he realized vaguely as he sipped the brandy. He should probably go to his suite and shower and change. There was even a smear of blood on his gray riding pants. Her blood. His grip tightened on the glass. Then he forced his hand to relax, one finger at a time. He had to keep his mind blank. Heaven knew when Madchen would see fit to come and give him the report on Pandora. If he let himself remember that nightmare moment when he'd found her lying crumpled on the stony mountain path, he'd go to pieces.

He couldn't do that. Pandora needed him to keep back the cold. Lord, he had felt as if he were bleeding inside when she murmured those poignant words. He was still bleeding. He leaned his head back and closed his eyes. He hadn't prayed since he was a child, but every breath he drew was a prayer now. Let her be well. Let him have the chance to keep his promise.

It was over two hours later when Madchen knocked, and then entered the library. Philip sat up straight. His shoulders were tense as he searched the doctor's face for any hint of expression. "Well?"

"There are no broken bones, as far as I can tell without an X ray." He nodded toward the cellarette. "May I have a drink?" he asked politely.

Philip made an impatient gesture. "Help yourself. What do you mean, as far as you can tell? Why didn't you take the X rays?"

"I thought it better not to, until I consulted you." Madchen was at the bar, pouring himself a small glass of white wine. "I wanted to determine your wishes in the matter."

"My wishes? What the hell do you mean? My 'wish' is to get your daughter well as quickly as possible. What the devil did you think I'd want?"

"There is no question that Pandora will be well in fairly short order." Madchen sipped the white wine with appreciation. "She has a very strong constitution. It's the child I'm wondering about. X rays would not be wise for the embryo."

Philip froze. "The child?"

"Pandora's approximately four weeks pregnant," Madchen said calmly. "She has had a bad fall. It will take extremely delicate handling to assure that the infant survives." He met Philip's eyes. "I wanted to be very sure that you wished me to take that care. After all, an illegitimate child can be very troublesome for a man in your position."

There was stunned silence in the room. "My God," Philip breathed incredulously. "She's your daughter."

Madchen shrugged. "An illegitimate child is often an inconvenience to the mother as well."

"You son of a bitch."

"There's no need to be abusive." Madchen straightened his horn-rimmed glasses. "I'm only looking out for your interests as my employer."

"What about her interests? You know damned well that Pandora would want that child." Philip could feel fury coursing through every vein. "You *know* that, damn your soul. Yet you're willing to take it from her while she's lying there helpless and unable to protect herself."

"I take it you want the child," Madchen said stolidly. "You had only to say so. Of course I'll make every effort to ensure a successful pregnancy."

"You're damn right, you will," Philip bit out. "You've cheated her out of affection all her life. You're not going to take this away from her too. You'll treat her as if a mere breath would shatter her." He rose to his feet, his hands clenched into fists. "And you'll be *nice* to her, or I'll tear you limb from limb."

Madchen blinked in surprise. "I've never been unkind to Pandora. I don't know what you mean."

Philip drew a deep breath and slowly unclenched his hands. It was obvious that Madchen was speaking the truth. He was an emotional cripple. Philip had to keep reminding himself of that or he would end up strangling the man. "Just make sure that you don't hurt her," he said as he turned away wearily. "Perhaps it would be better if you saw as little of her as possible."

"As you like." Madchen set his wineglass down on the cellarette. "I would like to call your attention to one point, however. I wasn't the one who was responsible for Pandora being in that first-aid room tonight." He looked up. "And I think perhaps you were, Sheikh El Kabbar."

Philip could feel the blood draining from his face. He felt a million years old. "You're right," he said bitterly. "Between us, we've nearly destroyed her. We should be very proud of ourselves." His hand was trembling as he raised it to cover his eyes. "She's probably the most loving human being either one of us will ever encounter, and we've managed to rip her to pieces." His hand dropped to his side.

"Well, it's up to us to put those pieces together again. I just hope to God she'll let us do it."

He sat down in his chair and picked up his brandy glass from the table. "Now, get back to Pandora and take care of her. If that baby dies, I'll break you, Madchen." He frowned. "Don't tell Pandora that she's pregnant. I'll do it myself. And for heaven's sake, if you can't say something kind to her, don't say anything at all."

Madchen moved ponderously toward the door. "Naturally I'll do everything I can. I told you that." He closed the door briskly behind him.

Philip leaned against the high back of the chair, his eyes staring blindly before him. A child. He had never thought about being a father. Yet there was no doubt he wanted Pandora's child. There was not a thing on God's green earth that he wouldn't cherish if it was loved and wanted by Pandora.

He wouldn't think of the pain or the difficulties to come. He wouldn't think of Madchen or of Pandora's white face when she had run out of the library earlier that evening. Instead, he would think of Pandora's child, even now growing in her womb. His child. He tested the idea and found it brought a sweeping rush of possessive joy. Yes, he would spend the time until he could go to Pandora thinking about their child.

EIGHT

PHILIP WAS LYING naked beside her, his arm heavy and possessive around her and his alert gaze on her face. Pandora was naked, too, but she couldn't seem to remember how she got that way. Had they been making love?

"Philip...?"

"Shh..." His lips touched hers in a quick, gentle kiss. "Go back to sleep. You need it. You're going to be as sore as hell in the morning."

"Why should I be..." Her eyes suddenly widened. "Oedipus! Is he all right?"

His lips tightened. "Better than you are. He just went for a midnight run."

"I fell off," she murmured, attempting to remember. "I tried to stop him, he reared, and I fell." Her eyes flew to his face. "Have I done something stupid to myself?"

"You mean like breaking your back?" His eyes flashed in the dim lamplight. "No, but you damn well could have. You're only suffering from shock and bruises. Your father said you were to stay in bed and take it easy for the next week or so."

"My father's been here? I don't remember that." She laughed shakily. "Are you sure I didn't hit my head as well?"

"I'm sure. You've just been sleeping like the dead. Shock, Madchen said." He raised himself on his elbow and the sheet fell to his waist, revealing the soft mat of dark hair that roughened his chest. "Sleep is the best thing for you right now. Your father said that if you woke and had problems I should give you a light sedative."

"I don't want to go back to sleep. I'm wide awake now." Her eyes traveled around the room. "This is your suite. What am I doing here?"

"I wanted you in here. Madchen's assistant is on the premises, but I wasn't about to let you spend the night in the first-aid room." He smiled with such warmth, she felt a momentary dizziness that had nothing to do with her fall. "I decided, very self-ishly, that I wouldn't be able to sleep without you tonight."

Her breath stopped in her lungs. "You appear to have been doing fine for the last month."

"I have?" His lips twisted ruefully. "I doubt if I got more than a few hours' sleep a night during the entire month. I've discovered that being in bed with you is very habit-forming." He bent forward and brushed her temple gently with his lips. "I may not ever be able to sleep without you again."

"Don't do this to me, Philip. I'm not a little girl to be given presents because I'm hurt." She glanced significantly at the door that led to the Khadim suite. "You weren't handing out any gifts earlier tonight." Her hand reached up to touch her throat, which felt naked without the medallion. "You were taking them away. Is Miss Lenat still here?"

His face tightened with pain, and she noticed for the first time how pale and haggard he looked. "No, she left almost immediately. Natalie isn't obtuse. She realized I was only using her as a way to hurt you." He removed his arm and rolled away from her. "She congratulated me on my ability to do that. She said that I had hurt you very much." He sat up on the side of the bed, his back turned to her. She couldn't see his face, but every muscle and tendon of his spine was taut with an agonizing tension. "She was right. I did it very well, didn't I?"

"Yes." Her voice was low. "You never do things halfway. I thought I was dying, and then I thought it would be better to die than to hurt that much."

He stood up and walked over to the chest across the room, his movements oddly jerky for a man so well coordinated. "You could have died." His voice was muffled. He took something from the top of the chest and was walking toward her again. His face was drawn, the skin pulled tightly over his high cheekbones. He knelt on the floor beside the bed. "I almost killed you."

"No, I was stupid," she said gently. "I shouldn't have let you drive me away like that. I thought I was so strong, but I seemed to break into a million pieces when you took my medallion away."

"God!" The exclamation was torn from him. He lifted her hand from the bed and laid the back of it against his cheek. "So did I." He rubbed her hand back and forth. His skin was slightly abrasive against the smoother flesh of her hand. "It was like dying or being born." He closed his eyes. "Maybe something like that did happen in the library tonight."

"I don't know what you mean."

"I mean I felt as if everything I'd ever known or believed about myself was suddenly torn away, leaving me naked and alone." He turned her hand over and pressed a kiss into her palm. "I'm going to have to start all over and I don't know how to go about it. Will you help me, Pandora?"

"What are you trying to tell me?" she whispered.

He laughed harshly. "I'm trying to tell you I love you. I'm not doing it very well, am I?"

Her eyes widened in shock. "You love . . ."

"I don't know why you're so surprised." His lips curved in a rueful smile. "You always told me that I did."

"I know I did," she said dazedly. "It's just that it's happened so fast. I have to think about it."

"Well, while you're thinking about it"—he raised his hand and slipped the medallion he held around her neck—"wear this. It belongs to you." His fingers fumbled with the catch. "It will always belong to you."

"No." She suddenly put her hand up to stop him. "I don't want to put it back on." She moistened her lips nervously. "Not right now."

He went still. "Why not?"

Her eyes held bewilderment and a hint of pain. "I'm not sure. I don't think I trust you, Philip."

He flinched as if she'd struck him. "I suppose I deserve that," he said hoarsely. "But I don't think I've ever told you anything but the truth." His lips twisted mirthlessly. "Except when I told you I didn't want you. I lied through my teeth about that."

Her gaze was grave. "No, you've never lied to me before, but I don't think you've ever felt this guilty before. You have the idea that you're responsible for what happened to me tonight. It's not true, but I think it's shaken you just the same."

"It *was* my fault, dammit. And I feel guilty as hell, but that doesn't have anything to do with what I'm telling you."

"Don't you see? I can't be sure of that." Her lips were trembling as she tried to smile. "I want to take you at your word, but I think I found out something tonight too."

His eyes darkened with sudden pain. "That you don't love me after all?"

"No, that will go on forever," she said quietly. "It's too much a part of me to ever stop." She drew a deep breath. "No, it was about myself that I learned something. I found out that loving you wasn't enough, that I had to love myself as well. Ever since I met you I've been trailing you like a shadow. I thought just being close to you would make me happy. But I found out tonight that wasn't true. I need you to love me as much as I love you." She lifted her chin. "I'm pretty damn special. I *deserve* to be loved."

"I do love you," Philip said with a frown. "What the devil do you think I've been saying?"

"I have to be sure. It would tear me apart if I was fooled into thinking pity and guilt were love. I would rather be without you entirely than have that happen."

"So what do we do now? Am I supposed to go out and fight a dragon to prove my love?"

"Well, perhaps just a little dragon." A tiny smile was tugging at her lips. "For you, it will probably be worse than slaying a dragon. I want you to wait. I want time to make sure that you're capable of giving me what I'll give you. I know how you usually go after whatever you want. Your campaigns resemble Alexander's conquest of Persia." She paused. "I don't want to be invaded. I want to make my own decision."

"The decision's made. I love you, you love me. Why be so stupid as to waste any more time?" He suddenly smiled with beguiling warmth. "Someone told me recently that we're not getting any younger."

"That someone did a lot of growing up tonight," she said soberly.

The smile faded from his face. He kissed her palm one more time before placing it on the bed. "Yes, I imagine you did," he said wearily. "All right, you'll have your time. I promise I won't push." His voice was suddenly fierce. "For now. But don't expect my patience to last forever. Two weeks and then the invasion begins." His eyes were narrowed and glittering on her face. "And I never particularly admired Alexander's campaign strategy. I always thought Hannibal's march across the Alps was much bolder and more innovative." He rose to his feet. "Two weeks. Then we'll be married and start living happily ever after."

"Married?" she asked faintly.

He frowned haughtily. "Of course, what else? I told you I loved you, didn't I?" He swung the golden medallion in his hand. "It's obvious that I'm going to need more than this to hold you from now on. We'll see what a marriage ceremony will do."

"*If* I decide to marry you," she said serenely, "it will be when I'm asked politely, not told."

"We'll see." He looked reckless. "I don't recall that Hannibal asked the Alps if they wanted to be crossed."

She shook her head resignedly. So much for Philip's chastened mood. "Philip..."

He shook his head. "Don't feel threatened. In two weeks I'll be Hannibal. Until then I'll be"—his eyes were suddenly dancing with mischief—"your Khadim."

"What!"

"Why not? I know the role well. I've studied it long enough." His tone was low and coaxing. "Would you like to have your own Khadim, Pandora?"

"Philip, stop joking."

He lifted mocking brows. "If you deserve to be loved, don't you think you deserve to be serviced by someone whose only desire is to please?" His eyes were holding hers intently. "Look at me, Pandora.

Do I please you? Did I please you that first night? I know I hurt you, but wasn't there a little pleasure too?"

"More than a little," she said huskily. "You know that."

"No, I don't know. I was in such a fever that I wasn't aware of anything but how you felt around me." His hand closed tightly on the medallion. "But I'll know next time. It's a Khadim's duty to put the client's pleasure first. I'll watch your face very closely while I move and thrust—"

"Philip!"

He chuckled. "Sorry, I forgot for a moment that you're still ill. You have that effect on me." He glanced down at himself with a rueful smile. "Among certain others." He suddenly frowned anxiously. "Do you need that sedative before I leave?"

She shook her head. "You're going?"

He bent forward to kiss her forehead. "Just next door. To the Khadim suite. I find that very appropriate, as well as less of a temptation. I'll look in on you later." He crossed the room, his carriage lithe and indomitably royal in his nudity.

"Philip."

He paused as he opened the door and looked over his shoulder inquiringly. "Yes?"

Her brow was knitted in a frown. "I was bleeding. I felt it as I was lying there. Are you sure I was just bruised?"

He hesitated. "You were badly jarred," he said. "But there's nothing to worry about. You'll be fine." He winked roguishly. "The word of a Khadim."

He didn't hear her low chuckle as he shut the door.

The first present came in the afternoon of the next day. It was a silver vase wrought with such exquisite workmanship, it was a sensuous pleasure to look at it. It was filled to overflowing with dozens of cream-colored roses touched at the heart with a delicate peach hue.

Raoul set it beside the bed on the rosewood night table. "From the Sheikh El Kabbar," he said formally. Then a puzzled frown wrinkled his brow. "With the compliments of your Khadim."

There was a gift every day after that. They ranged from a hi-fi video recorder with a complete library of films to a comb and brush set of white jade embedded with amethysts in a beautiful floral design.

"Are you trying to overwhelm me?" she asked with a grin when Philip came into the room on the afternoon the comb and brush set arrived. "If you are, you're succeeding." Her finger traced the amethyst motif on the back of the brush. "But I think you've got our roles reversed. It's the client who is supposed to give the gifts."

He sat down on the bed beside her and took the brush from her hand. "I look at the broader picture. A Khadim is supposed to give pleasure. I'm limited at present as to the kind of pleasure I can give you, so I decided to improvise. The gifts do please you, don't they?"

"Of course they do, but..."

"Then that's all that's important. I'm obviously a tremendous success in my new role." He placed another pillow behind her back and eased her into a sitting position. "Besides, the giving of every gift has a selfish motive too." He moved to a position at the head of the bed behind her. "You know how self-indulgent I am."

He began pulling the brush through her hair with long, slow strokes. "I've looked forward to doing this ever since I ordered it from Rome. I love touching your hair." His other hand tangled in its thick length. "It's so silky and warm and alive. It makes my fingers tingle slightly as I draw them through. Are you enjoying this too?"

Her head was bent forward, her eyes half closed. If she were a cat, she would have purred. "It's wonderful," she said drowsily. He'd been at the stables. She could detect the scents of horse and leather and fresh air that surrounded him. "Have you been riding Oedipus?"

"Yes." The brush was at her temple, sweeping up and then down, the bristles massaging her scalp and tugging at the tresses in a blissfully sensuous fashion. "He's as temperamental as ever. He tried to run under a low-hanging branch and knock me off. He's nothing if not a challenge."

"He just has a strong personality," she protested. "He wanted to keep you on your toes."

"No, he wanted to knock me on my backside. There's a big difference." The stroking of the brush slowed. "You've been very meek about staying in bed for the last few days. How are you feeling?"

"Sore." She made a face. "For some reason, I can't seem to keep awake. I've been napping half the day away. I suppose it must be the shock."

"Probably." He carefully brushed her hair to one side and kissed the nape of her neck. "I expect it will pass shortly. Has your father been in to see you?"

She shook her head. "His assistant has been coming in every day and reporting back to him. I understand I'm to be honored with a visit before I'm allowed to resume normal activities."

"Does it bother you that he hasn't come?"

She thought about it. "No," she said slowly. "I think I've come to terms with my father." She laughed shakily. "It's about time, isn't it?"

"I'm glad." He was silent a moment. "I received a follow-up report on you from the detective agency this morning. It was very interesting."

"Was it?" She leaned back against him dreamily. "Have you ever considered the possibility that your avid interest in my scandalous past may be slightly unhealthy?"

"Scandalous, hell," he growled. "Poor little greedy rock star whose passion for luxuries impoverished her and forced her into a life of sin."

"I am impoverished," she said lightly. "I'm sure your Sherlock discovered that when he was nosing around."

"Oh, yes. Your bank account is bare as a bone. Denbrook found that out at once." He paused. "It took him longer to find out where the money had gone."

"Really? And I thought he appeared to be such an efficient operator."

"He was looking for investments, not charities. You gave last year's entire income to the Ethiopian Relief Fund. The year before you set up a shelter for stray animals in upper New York State."

"I like animals," she said. "And I didn't need the money. I was on the road all the time."

"So you gave it all away. Then you threw your career down the drain to come with me here to Sedikhan." His tone was suddenly harsh. "For heaven's sake, don't you have any sense of self-preservation?"

"I do not," she said quietly. "You taught it to me."

There was a silence in which the only sound was the sibilant hiss of the brush moving through her hair. "I know I did." His words were low and halting. "I don't give gentle lessons, do I?"

She didn't answer. She felt an aching need to ease the torment she sensed beneath his question, but the pain of that night was still too fresh, Philip's cruelty still too incomprehensible to give him false assurances.

He pulled the strap of her blue nightgown off her shoulder and placed a kiss where her arm joined the shoulder. "I like this spot," he murmured. "I can feel the suppleness of your muscles beneath the satin skin." He nipped the flesh lightly. "It's very arousing."

Yes, it was. Pandora could feel the heat tingle through her shoulder. She felt warm and lazy and infinitely treasured. How odd that those feelings could exist side by side with this tingling heat. "Philip, I don't think—"

"It's all right." His lips moved to the hollow at the base of her throat. "We're just playing a little. I know you're not well enough to"—he suddenly chuckled as he repeated her phrase—"be invaded."

"I remember the last time you 'played,' " she said breathlessly.

"That was different. That was the preliminary for the invasion." He slipped the strap from her other shoulder. "This is just me giving you pleasure. Just a little, not enough to make you ache as I've been doing for the last few days."

"Have you?" she asked with a twinge of guilt. She knew Philip was a highly sexed man, yet she had been accepting his services as if he were a maid. He had bathed her, helped her to the bathroom, kept her company, and sought to entertain her almost all of her waking hours since the night of the accident. "Perhaps you could arrange for someone else to help me for a few days. I'll be all right after that."

"I want to do it." He was brushing her hair again. "I'm enjoying it in a masochistic way. You're my hair shirt."

"Well, then I guess I don't have to worry about you. There's nothing in the least erotic about a hair shirt."

"How do you know?" His lips were moving back and forth on her neck. "Any texture can be erotic, depending on the way it's used." His arms were sliding around her. "For instance, do you know what I told the jeweler when I ordered this hairbrush? I told him to make the bristles firm, but soft as a whisper."

"You did?" His hard chest was pressing against her back and his warm breath was feathering her ear.

"Shall we see if he carried out my instructions?" He pushed the bodice of her gown down, baring her breasts, and ran the brush lightly over one taut mound. The sensation of the soft bristles moving across her sensitive flesh was incredible. She drew in her breath sharply, and heard him laugh softly in her ear. "Textures. How does it feel?" He brushed lightly back and forth with a teasing stroke that suddenly caused her to arch forward against his arms with a little cry.

His long, strong fingers pressed lightly below her left breast. "Your heart is going wild. I don't think you have to answer." He kissed her temple, pulled up the bodice of the gown, and slipped the thin straps over her shoulders. "I'll send the jeweler a little bonus. I'll have to remember that you like that particular texture." He reached over and set the brush on the bedside table. Then his arms were cradling her again, pulling her back against his chest and rocking her as if she were a child in need of soothing. "Now just relax and we'll cuddle like this for a while." There were long, peaceful moments in which the haze of sensuality that engulfed her was gradually transformed into warm contentment. "I do love you, you know." His voice was low and clear in her ear.

"Oh, I do hope you do," she whispered. He was so dear. She had never dreamed that he could be this

Iris Johansen

exquisitely gentle. "I love you so much, Philip. I don't want to leave you. I never want to leave you."

He stiffened against her. "You're never going to leave me. Stop talking about it." His arms tightened, and then released her. He stood up.

"You're going?" she asked, disappointed.

"I think I'd better." His lips twisted in a lopsided grin. "I need some more exercise. I get a little too anxious to start climbing those Alps when you say things like that. I'm riding out to the irrigation project for an hour or so. I'll have Raoul look in on you every so often until I get back."

"When will that be?" she asked wistfully. "Will you be back in time for dinner?"

"I wouldn't miss it," he said with a smile that lit his dark face. "Wait for me." He strode toward the door. "Do you want to nap, or shall I put a movie on the video recorder?"

"A movie, I think. Something funny."

He inserted a cassette and turned on the television. "There, that should keep you occupied." He slanted her a mischievous glance over his shoulder. "There are a few X-rated ones in the collection, but

I thought we'd save those to watch together. I want to see if you're as responsive to visual stimuli as you are to touch."

"I think we'll wait on those," she said dryly. "I've had quite enough stimuli, thank you."

"Pandora," he said softly as he opened the door. "You have no idea yet how much is enough. But you will, love. You will."

The gown was delivered the afternoon before Philip's two-week hiatus was over. When she opened the box the first thing she was conscious of was the color. The deep cranberry of the brocade was so vibrant it appeared to glow with jewel-like radiance in its nest of white tissue paper.

The design of the gown was very simple. The boat neckline and the long, full sleeves were both modest, but the bodice would cling to her breasts with loving detail. The high waist that started immediately beneath the bust flowed to the floor with a gentle flare.

She picked up the card lying on top of the gown.

"It's copied from an authentic bedouin wedding robe," she read. "The brocade was my idea. Though wool is the traditional fabric, I want all the textures to be right tonight when you wear this."

Her lips curved in a smile as she picked up the gown and held it at arm's length to look at it. Philip and his textures. He wouldn't be able to complain about this particular brocade. It was both soft and supple, and a pleasure to touch.

That Philip did intend to touch tonight was clear, and the knowledge sent a little tingle of shock through her. It shouldn't have. The sexual tension between them had been evident in every minute of their time together. Yet these two weeks had possessed the misty aura of a dream. Philip had been so gentle. Gentle and sweet and loving, so very loving. And now that loving was going to blossom into physical fulfillment. Their joining would be as natural and beautiful as the time that had gone before. She felt a sudden surge of excitement rising within her. It was like the moment before a jump, when there was only the sky before her and the unknown on the other side. Evidently Philip had decided to start his campaign early.

She experienced a thrill of happiness. It was time to move out of the dream into reality, and she was ready for it. She whirled around in a circle, hugging the gown to her. Oh yes, she was ready for it.

Philip didn't join her for dinner that night. She was standing on the balcony perhaps fifteen minutes after her tray had been taken away, trying to calm the butterflies in her stomach, when she heard the closing of the door.

"Come in and let me look at you." Philip was standing in the doorway of the balcony as she turned. He was dressed in white. Superbly fitted white trousers clung to his narrow waist and slim hips, and his white, long-sleeved shirt was fashioned of a material that glowed with a soft, silky luster in the darkness. "I waited too long. It's too dark out here to see you."

"I was wondering if you were coming at all," she said lightly as she moved toward him. "You didn't show up for dinner."

"I learned my lesson the last time," he said. "I

had only two days of anticipation to go through before that first night, and I nearly went crazy. I would have been tempted to toss the tray off the balcony tonight."

"Me too."

He went still. "You mean that? I was afraid you'd think I was rushing you."

"Well, a little, maybe." She smiled teasingly. "Tomorrow was the day for Hannibal's arrival."

"It still is." He drew her into the room and shut the balcony doors behind them. "This is still a Khadim night. I promise you. Stay here while I turn on the light."

He was gone, a pale ghost in a darkly shadowed room. Then the soft glow of the bedside lamp illuminated the darkness as he turned to look at her.

"Oh yes," he said after a long moment. "I knew you'd look like that in the gown. The richest of wine and the most shimmering of silver-gold. There's nothing more beautiful on the face of the earth."

"I love it," she said. "It makes me feel like a princess."

"Every bride should feel like that." He was moving back to stand before her. "And that is a bridal outfit, Pandora." He cupped her face in his two hands. "Why not take advantage of it?" His lips were hovering near hers. "We could be married tonight. Why don't we fly to Marasef and get the formalities out of the way? You know you're going to do it anyway."

"Probably," she said huskily. He was so near. The warm scent of spice and soap was enveloping her, and his eyes were almost mesmerizing.

"Not probably. It's a certainty." His fingers were on her shoulders, kneading the flesh through the supple brocade. "Haven't you kept me dangling long enough?"

"I wouldn't play games like that. It's just that it's so important that I be sure."

"Yes, I know." His teeth nipped gently at her lower lip. "I wish I didn't. It would be so much easier just to rush you off your feet." He chuckled. "Well, there's one way I can whisk you off your feet."

He suddenly picked her up and carried her

toward the bed, his face alight with laughter as he looked down at her. "I'm giving you fair warning. By morning I have every intention of wresting that promise from you." He laid her down in a flurry of cranberry brocade. "I'm going to be such a very seductive Khadim that you're never going to want to do without me again."

"That's no challenge. I don't want to do without you now."

His face was beautifully tender as he gently brushed back a lock of hair from her face. "Then you realize how simple everything is. Neither one of us will be without the other from now on. Turn over, love, and let me get you out of this thing."

She rolled over on her stomach. "It's not a thing, it's beautiful." She heard the hiss of the long zipper and then felt a breath of cool air on her naked back. She heard him inhale sharply. "I see you don't believe in wasting time either." His palm reached out to cover the smooth curve of her buttocks. "Lord, that's pretty."

"I told you I didn't play games."

"Then I'll have to teach you. Certain games are

very enjoyable." He was deftly slipping her arms out of the sleeves. "I'm sure you'd be better at them than you are at mah-jongg."

"I'd have to be," she muttered. "It's an idiotic game anyw—" She gasped as she felt his warm lips at the hollow of her back. When she got her breath back she asked, "Is that a fair move?"

"If you like it." His teeth gently nipped the soft flesh below the hollow. "Tell me what you like and I'll make up new rules as we go along."

"You always do," she said with amusement. "Ouch!" That bite had been decidedly more punishing than the last. "You did have dinner, didn't you?"

"No." The lightness was completely gone from his voice. "I couldn't eat. I couldn't sleep last night. Sometimes I wonder if I'm ever going to be able to do either again." His hands were running up and down her back in long, caressing strokes, savoring the silkiness of her flesh. "I'm tired of keeping things light. I don't feel light, dammit! I feel serious as hell."

He was lifting her, turning her over on the rumpled cranberry brocade. She was startled when she saw the intense look of hunger on his face. "No seduction?" she asked softly.

"I'm trying." His gaze was traveling over her, finally fastening on the soft golden nest of her womanhood. "It's never been so difficult with any other woman." He lowered his cheek and rubbed it against her belly. The slight abrasion caused her muscles to contract, and her hands went involuntarily to his shoulders. "It was a game with them. Skill against skill." His warm breath was searing her. "I want to make it so good for you and I'm afraid I'll foul it up." Her heart was pounding wildly, and she felt a burning begin between her thighs. "This *means* something to me."

"It means something to me too." Her heart jerked as his lips moved against her in the most intimate of kisses. "Philip!"

"You're so sweet here," he said as his hands cupped her gently. "But then, every part of you is sweet. Do you know how beautiful you are?"

Her hands clenched on his shoulders, her nails

digging into the silk of his shirt. "Yes. No. What did you say?" His tongue touched her, and she arched up against him with a little cry.

He raised his head. "I love to hear you cry out like that, but it makes it hard as the devil to hold on." He lowered his lips to kiss her hand, which was still clenching desperately at his shoulders. "But it bothers me that you seem confused about how lovely you are. I think we should clear that up once and for all." He stood and pulled her to her feet. "Come on." He propelled her across the room, ignoring her confusion as he whisked her into the Khadim suite.

"Philip, I don't understand—" She broke off. They were before a floor-length triple mirror that was standing upright against the wall. The lamps were off in the suite and the only light was that streaming from Philip's room. It came as a little shock to see her own slim nudity offset by Philip's fully clothed figure behind her.

"I remembered how excited you were in the dressing room." Philip's arms slid around her waist. "I thought you might like this." His hands slid down to slowly massage her belly. "The night I had it installed I lay in that bed just looking at it, imagining how you'd look standing here surrounded on three sides by mirrors. Do you know what that did to me?" He lowered his head to whisper in her ear. "I was hurting so much that I wanted to run to you and bury myself in you and stay forever. I've ached like that every night since then." One hand had left her and begun to unbutton his white silk shirt. She could see the tanned flesh and the dark triangle of hair on his chest emerging from the opening in the shirt, and her eyes clung helplessly. The hard, impersonal sheen of the glass contrasted with the intimate picture it was reflecting and the explosive emotions seething between them.

"See how pretty you are." His hand was tanned and graceful as it moved up to cup her breast, surrounding and lifting it. "This is what I see when I look at you. All this sweet firmness." He pinched the pink crown with thumb and forefinger. "This lovely budding."

"I feel distinctly narcissistic." She laughed shakily as she leaned back against him. "I think I'm embarrassed." The hair on his chest brushed her naked spine and her knees began to feel as if they wouldn't hold her up.

"You shouldn't be." His hand dropped away from her as he shrugged out of his shirt and it dropped to the floor. "Are you embarrassed looking at me?"

"No." He was a beautiful shadow figure, his supple bronze muscles silhouetted by the light, which also picked up the luster of his coal black hair. "I like to look at you."

"Then we'd better make things more equal." His hands were working swiftly at his belt. She watched dreamily as he stripped off the remainder of his clothes, tossing them in a careless heap on top of his shirt. "There, now we're even. Does that make you feel better?"

She didn't know how she felt. Electricity was arcing through her, swirling about her. His hands were running over her, pausing every now and then to stroke, weigh, twine, and rub with sensual enjoyment. Her breath was coming in little jerks as her gaze clung to the mirror reflection of his narrowed eyes.

She could feel his hard arousal pressed against her, and his chest was moving heavily with the harshness of his breathing. His hands suddenly stilled on her body, and she could feel the shudder that racked him. His lips were a thin line of tension. "It's gone on too long. I can't wait any longer."

"Then don't wait." Her voice was trembling. Her entire body was trembling. "I can't wait either. Let's ... go to bed."

He made a sound deep in his throat. "I can't wait for that either." He suddenly spun her around, lifting her, parting her legs, and wrapping them around his hips. "Hold on to me." He was searching, finding, and then plunging with one deep stroke into the heart of her.

She cried out, her fingers digging into his shoulders. He was moving, his hands cupping her bottom for even deeper penetration. "Closer," he muttered. "I can't get close enough to you." His hips bucked rhythmically, and she bit her lip, trying to stifle a moan. He lifted his eyes to the mirror. "*Mine.*

You're mine." His hips moved again. "Say it, Pandora."

"Yes," she whispered. So full. Fire, sensation, an aching need for more.

One hand lifted to tangle in her hair and tilt back her head so he could look into her eyes. "You're going to belong to me forever. There will be no more talk about going away." His lips covered hers with a passion that contained an element of leashed savagery. His tongue entered, ravaged, possessed. *She* was possessed, a part of him, both physically and emotionally.

His head lifted and his nostrils flared in an effort to get his breath. "I'll never let you leave me now."

His arms were about her again and he was turning, walking toward the bed. She gasped. He looked down at her with a faint smile. "You like this? I thought you would." He sat down on the edge of the bed. His hands ran up and down her back, touching, exploring, savoring the smoothness of her. "You always did enjoy a good ride."

He was lying back on the bed, his hands on her hips. "Do I remind you of Oedipus now, love?"

Then he was moving, thrusting, watching her to detect every ripple of pleasure that crossed her face. "Do I?" he repeated.

"No." The tension was building to such a fantastic degree that she scarcely realized what she was saying. "You're wilder." He thrust deeper, and a shiver of pleasure ran through her. "Much wilder."

"I told you that you didn't really know either one of us." His palms moved up to cover her breasts. "But you're learning fast. Hold on, love, we're going for the jump."

The approach was dizzying, and the jump itself incredible. They soared into the stratosphere and beyond. Exhilaration, beauty, reaching for the sky. Then they *owned* the sky as no one ever had before.

Her cheek was pressed to Philip's chest and his arms were holding her with such force she could scarcely breathe. His heart was pounding so hard it seemed to be trying to burst through the wall of his chest. "Are you okay?" she asked.

He laughed. "That's what I'm supposed to ask." He kissed her gently. "Yes, I am most certainly okay. I've never been better."

She suddenly giggled. "I'm sure that's true, but it's immodest of you to say so." She started to move out of his arms. "I'm too heavy for you. Let me go."

"No." His grip tightened around her. His tone was suddenly intense. "Stay. Stay forever."

"That might be a little awkward for you." She bent down and kissed him lovingly. "Though I'd be more than willing."

"I'll have to think about it." He rolled over, still holding her close. "There has to be a way."

She nestled nearer, her cheek finding the hollow of his shoulder. This deep contentment was almost as wonderful as the passion that had gone before. "I like this. The night of the dinner party you held me like this, but I fell asleep. Pinch me if I do it tonight. I want to enjoy every moment."

Tenderness swept over him, and he felt his throat tighten painfully. He hadn't realized how much he had missed her joyful eagerness. There had been an underlying element of reserve and uncertainty about Pandora since the night of the accident. He had been unable to overcome that withdrawal, no matter how hard he tried. He brushed his lips across the top of her head. "I refuse to pinch you, but I promise I'll find ways to keep you awake." His hand reached up to stroke the curve of her cheek. "Very enjoyable ways."

"That sounds nice, but you'll have to be pretty quick about it," she said drowsily. "I can't seem to stay awake for long these days. Maybe I should get some vitamins."

"What a demanding wench. I'll try my best to oblige." His index finger smoothed her brow. "And I'll stuff you so full of vitamins you'll be even more demanding..." He paused. "When we get back from Marasef tomorrow."

A wedding in Marasef. At this beautiful moment it appeared wildly appealing. "You have superb timing. I'd fly to the moon with you if you asked me right now."

"Marasef will do. Raoul will have them ready the plane as soon as we wake in the morning."

"Why do I feel the invasion has already started?"

"No invasion. I'm wooing you," he said with indignation. "Can't you tell the difference? You can't deny that my wooing was successful tonight?"

"No, I can't deny it," she said quietly. "But we both agreed that sex wasn't love."

His hand moved from her cheek to tilt her chin up. "That wasn't sex, that *was* love. You know it as well as I do. If you're not sure that I love you now, what makes you think you'll be sure next week or even next year? We could be candidates for geriatric care before you decide to take a chance on me again. Why don't you admit—"

"All right."

He frowned. "All right what?"

"All right, I'll marry you. Marasef seems like an ideal place. I'll wear my bedouin wedding robe and—"

He stopped her with his lips, and when he lifted his head his eyes were glittering like turquoise beneath the sea. "You won't be sorry. I promise you, you won't be sorry as long as you live."

"I don't think I will." Hope was growing, along with a wild joy. She had kept that hope firmly suppressed in the past weeks, afraid that it would never be fulfilled. Now she felt as if it had unfurled like a bright banner within her. "Oh, Philip, I do love you so much." She hugged him with all her strength, pressing quick, loving kisses on his entire face and throat. "I feel like swinging from a trapeze, or dancing, or belting out a gospel song."

He was laughing helplessly, and in that moment he looked almost boyish. "You don't need vitamins. But I may, if I'm going to keep up with you. I can't supply you with any of those amusements, but if you'll hush, I'll try to give you an alternative."

"What alternative?"

"One you appeared to like very much before." He kissed her lightly on the tip of her nose. "In short, I'm ready to oblige my very demanding wench."

She grinned as she snuggled against him happily. "Well, why didn't you say so? That's more fun anyway. What are we going to do this ti—"

Her question was lost as he began to demonstrate.

NINE

IT WAS LATE the next afternoon when the limousine pulled into the compound. The desert heat was oppressive, as it always was at that time of day, but Pandora was barely conscious of it. "Does Raoul know that I'm now an official thorn in his flesh?" She jumped out of the car before the driver could come around to open the door. "Do you think he'll quit and leave in a huff? That would be terrible, wouldn't it? You'd probably divorce me." She went into Philip's arms as Philip got out of the car.

"Wasn't it nice of Alex Ben Raschid and Sabrina to give us that lovely luncheon? I like them so much, don't you?"

He chuckled as his arms went around her. "Pandora, you're a bundle of energy. You've been running in high gear ever since we left for Marasef this morning."

"I'm happy," she said simply, her face glowing radiantly. "So happy, I feel as if the whole world is spinning like a beautiful pinwheel. *My* pinwheel."

He was silent for a moment, his face buried in the hair at her temple. "It's yours, if you want it," he said gruffly. "If you want the whole damn world, I'll find a way of getting it for you." He drew back and smiled with rare gentleness. "What do you want, Pandora?"

She shook her head. "Nothing. Why should I want anything more?" She made a face. "Except, perhaps, Raoul's blessing. Did you tell him we were going to be married today?"

Philip motioned for the driver to leave and took her elbow. "Yes," he said as he propelled her up the steps. "And you'll be astounded to know that he didn't give notice immediately. He said he believed that he had become accustomed to the catastrophes that surround you, and he would, on no account, desert me in my time of need." His eyes were twinkling. "I think he regards you as his greatest challenge."

"He likes me," Pandora said cheerfully. "He'll get used to the hullabaloo in time." She stopped on the top step, a sudden frown creasing her brow. "You're not going to want me to change, are you? Are you going to expect dignity and serenity now that I'm the lady of the house?"

His brows lifted. "Dignity and serenity from you? Hardly. I'll immediately have you committed if you develop either of those qualities. The best I can hope for are brief interludes in between the storms."

Her expression was clouding. "Am I that bad? I don't want to make life uncomfortable for you. Perhaps I could try to—"

He held up his hand. "Don't try. Like Raoul, I've become accustomed to living in the middle of a tempest. I'd probably find serenity hellishly boring after the past weeks." There was a teasing glint in his eye. "I demand even less of my wife than of my friends." He waved his hand magnanimously. "If you wish to bring another cobra into my salon, feel free."

"Well, now that you mention it, I've been wanting to talk to you about Beldar and Hanar. Don't you think we could—"

The door swung open.

"Saved in the nick of time," Philip said in an undertone as Raoul stepped aside to allow them to enter. "Though only temporarily, I'm sure."

There was a warm smile on Raoul's face. "May I offer my most sincere best wishes?" he asked as he closed the door behind them. "I've put a magnum of champagne on ice. I thought that would be in order."

"Thank you, Raoul." Pandora gave him a brilliant smile. "Champagne would be very fitting." Her eyes were sparkling with mischief. "See, I do recognize proper decorum every now and then."

"Recognizing is not performing," Raoul said with a tiny smile. "But then, the wife of Sheikh El Kabbar

will not have to obey rules. She can make her own.
It is for you to decide what is fitting." He bowed
slightly. "Will you have dinner in your suite or in
the dining room?"

"Neither." Pandora turned eagerly to Philip.
"Let's ride up into the hills and have a picnic. I can't
stand being cooped up anymore. I haven't been
out of that room for two weeks, except to go to
Marasef today."

"Why not?" Philip smiled indulgently. He released her elbow and turned to Raoul. "A picnic
supper then. Phone the stables and have our horses
saddled in about thirty minutes." He turned back to
Pandora. "We are going to take time to change out
of our bridal finery?"

"You look wonderful in white," she said idly.
The faultless tailoring of his white suit gave his
lean, powerful body an elegant panache. "I hate for
you to take it off."

His dark eyes were limpid as he gazed at her. "I
assure you, I'm looking forward to it exceedingly."

There was a sound from Raoul that was halfway
between a chuckle and a cough. He turned away.

"I'll make the arrangements at once," he said with sedate dignity. He abruptly turned back with a frown. "I'm extremely sorry. It completely slipped my mind. Dr. Madchen is waiting in the first-aid room. He's been there for over an hour."

"Really?" She felt Philip stiffen beside her, and she smiled reassuringly. It was sweet of him to be so protective, but not even an encounter with her father could dampen her spirits today. "Did you tell him why we were in Marasef?"

"Yes, of course." Raoul's lips tightened. "I also told him it was a most inconvenient time for an examination, but he insisted. He's going away to Munich on vacation tomorrow and wants to tidy up all the loose ends."

A loose end. How like her father to describe her in those terms. For an instant Pandora felt a familiar twinge, but instantly dismissed it. "Well, we wouldn't want to mess up his neat, tidy schedule," she said with careful lightness. "I'll see him, of course. Perhaps you'd better tell the grooms it will be an hour instead of thirty minutes."

"You don't have to see him," Philip said quietly.

"I'll go and explain that it's not a good time. He can see you when he comes back."

She shook her head. "I'll tell him I don't have time for a complete examination. Maybe if I let him see how well I look, he'll be happy with a token checkup." She smiled. "It will be fine. The world's my pinwheel today. Remember?" She started down the hall in the direction of the first-aid room. "I'll meet you in the suite when I've finished."

Karl Madchen was sitting at the desk in the first-aid room, a cup of tea in his hand, his gaze on the medical journal on the blotter before him. He looked up abstractedly as she came into the room. "Good afternoon, Pandora. Sit down on the examining table. I'll be with you as soon as I finish this paragraph."

The pinwheel slowed slightly in its giddy spinning, as if the wind had suddenly lessened.

She lifted her chin and moved decisively across the room. She hopped on the table, smoothing her cranberry brocade skirt against the sterile dark blue plastic. "Sure, take your time." She swung her feet idly as she glanced around the room. It looked as sterile as the examining table on which she was sitting, and she felt a sudden chill.

Her father was rising from the chair and crossing the room. "That's a very pretty dress," he said, "but I'm afraid you'll have to take it off. I want this examination to be fairly complete, since I'll be away for over a month." He took a stethoscope from the drawer of the cabinet beside the table. "My assistant informs me you're fully recovered now."

"I am. I feel wonderful," she said brightly. "So there's no need for a complete exam. I just came to show you how well I'm doing." She paused deliberately. "And to receive your best wishes. I was married today."

"Raoul told me. Congratulations. That was quite a coup. I would never have suspected that a person of your impulsive nature would have had the patience to plan a maneuver like this."

Congratulations, not best wishes. The pinwheel design was visible now, the movement sluggish. "Maneuver?"

"Is the soreness completely gone?" He picked up

her wrist, his gaze on his watch as he took her pulse. "No more bleeding?"

"No, not since the night of the fall."

"Are you experiencing any lack of energy or nausea?"

"No nausea. I've been very sleepy lately." She smiled. "I thought I'd ask you for some vitamins."

"Yes, of course. I'll leave a supply of multivitamins and iron tablets here in the cabinet. However, the drowsiness would have passed shortly even without them."

"I would have thought I'd be completely over the shock by now."

"Oh, you are. You're fully recovered from the accident. The drowsiness is merely because of the child."

"The child?" she repeated with numb lips.

He was reaching into a drawer and extracting a blood pressure gauge. "You may experience some morning sickness during the next month. It's not uncommon during the second and third months of pregnancy. I'll leave you pills for that as well." He glanced up with a frown as he unrolled the bandage. "I do wish you would permit me to give you a thorough examination before I leave Sedikhan. Sheikh El Kabbar was most concerned about the safety of his child. I wouldn't like him to think I've been derelict in my duty."

The pinwheel shuddered to a stop. It didn't matter. It was suddenly only a tawdry toy anyway.

"He was concerned?"

"Of course." He was rolling up the long sleeve of her gown, not looking at her. "We both know how possessive the man is. Naturally he would be worried about his first child and heir. Why else would he rush you out of your sick bed to ensure the child's legitimacy?"

Breathtaking agony. "No reason that I can think of." Her voice was almost steady, she noticed. How odd, when the world was crumbling all about her.

He was winding the pressure gauge around her upper arm. "It was clever of you to play upon his possessiveness to get what you wanted. I was surprised to hear that the sheikh had decided to—"

"Shut up!" Her voice wasn't steady any longer. It was shaking with an agony and a wild rage that seemed to fill the universe. "I don't want to hear any more!" She jumped to the floor, fumbling with the gauge on her arm. "Go away. Go to Munich, or go to hell. I don't care which." She had at last gotten the bandage off and she threw it on the floor. *"Just stay away from me!"*

She was running toward the door, trying to escape the cold, sterile room. Not that there was any place to run. The rest of the world was cold and sterile too. Tears were blinding her, and she didn't see Philip until she ran into him in the hall just outside the door. His arms closed around her, steadying her. "Whoa! You always go at everything full steam..." The smile faded as he looked down into her face. "Pandora?"

She tore herself away. "*Damn you.* Damn you to hell, Philip!" Her eyes were blazing in her white face. "I could kill you." Then she was running down the hall away from him.

Philip's hands clenched into fists at his sides. He muttered a vicious oath as he threw open the door to the first-aid room.

Madchen was kneeling to pick up a pressure gauge that lay on the floor, appearing as impassive as ever. "You told her," Philip said with barely controlled ferocity. "You *told* her, dammit."

"Not intentionally. Naturally I thought she'd know by now." Madchen rose to his feet and straightened his spectacles. "It's been over two weeks, and I thought surely you would have discussed the birth of the child. How else could she have persuaded you to marry her?"

"Persuaded *me*?" Philip drew a deep breath and tried to control the rage that was flowing through him. He wanted to murder the son of a bitch. "No, I hadn't told her yet. I was going to do it in the next few days. But you blew it. You blew it to hell, didn't you?"

"I'm extremely sorry. If I'd known, I assure you I wouldn't have—"

"You don't have the emotional capacity even for regret, Madchen," Philip bit out. "Get the hell out of Sedikhan. Don't take a month, take six months." He turned on his heel. "By then I may be able to look at you without wanting to strangle you. It's not likely, but there's a possibility."

The door slammed behind him.

Pandora didn't look up from her packing as Philip came into the room. She had changed into jeans and a yellow tunic top, but her feet were still bare. The brocade dress was tossed into a silken heap on the bed beside the open suitcase. "You can stop packing," Philip said. "You aren't going anywhere."

"Don't worry. I'm not taking any of your expensive bribes," she said jerkily. "I'm only taking what I came with. I'm sure you have no use for an orange wig." She sat down on the bed and began to put on her white tennis shoes. "And it might come in handy for me."

"You're not going anywhere," he repeated grimly. For the first time she noticed he had changed from his white suit into black riding pants and a black sweat shirt. The somber color accentuated his air of menace.

"The hell I'm not." She tied the lace of the second shoe and stood up. "I'm going far and I'm going fast. If you don't want me to use the plane or the car, I'll walk." She slammed the lid of the suitcase shut and fastened it. "Or hitchhike."

"You're upset. I know that. Will you please listen to me?" He came toward her. "I don't know what your lovable father said to you, but I'm sure it was expressed in the worst possible terms. He has a talent that way."

She whipped around to face him, flags of color suddenly flying in her pale cheeks. "He didn't try to present it any way at all. He just told me the cold facts. I'm going to have a child. Too bad neither one of you thought to inform me."

"There were reasons. If you'll calm down, I'll tell you what they were."

"I know what they were. I thought that you might be feeling sorry for me, but it was more than that, wasn't it?" Her eyes blazed up at him. "I was carrying your child. That made all the difference. You couldn't let me leave once you knew that. It would have offended your every instinct."

"You don't know what you're talking about," he said roughly.

"Don't I?" She smiled bitterly. "I thought your about-face was a little too good to be true. I guess I wanted to believe it so desperately that I let you convince me. You were very plausible, Philip. I swallowed the big lie without even batting an eye."

"I didn't lie," he said between his teeth. "I don't lie, dammit. I just didn't let you know the whole truth. I was going to tell you soon, but I was afraid you'd react like this."

"So you decided to secure the fortress before you let me in on the secret. Didn't it occur to you that I had a right to know about the child before I married you?"

"It occurred to me. I suppose I was just too scared to risk it."

"You should have been afraid. I never would have married you." Her hands clenched at her sides. "You had no right to fool me like that."

"Perhaps not, but I took that right anyway." His lips twisted. "I assume you think you're going to run back to your rock group and file for divorce now?"

"With the speed of light. I'll be free so fast it will make your head swim."

"No!" he said with great precision. "There will be no divorce and no running away. You're not leaving."

"The devil I'm not. You'll have to throw me into the dungeon to keep me here."

"That won't be necessary. The dungeon is very dirty and uncomfortable, as it hasn't been used for a century or so. I think house arrest will do as well. I'll even extend your privileges to the stables as long as you understand that you won't be permitted to ride."

She was staring at him incredulously. "You can't be serious."

"Oh yes, I'm very serious." His smile was bittersweet. "You told me once I was a good deal like my father. Perhaps you were right. He imprisoned my mother for nine months before his child was born. Believe me, I'll do the same if I have to."

"You're barbaric," she whispered.

"But then, you've always known that." His lips were a thin line. "You should have expected me to react like this. I'm not letting you leave here. When you calm down we'll talk."

"We have talked."

"You've done all the talking. I haven't even been permitted to defend myself." He turned away. "When I leave this room I'm giving orders that you're not to leave the premises. There will be guards posted throughout the house and in the courtyard. Your freedom won't be circumscribed unless you try to leave the grounds." He glanced over his shoulder, and for a moment his eyes were bright with pain. "When you're ready to let me explain, send for me. I'll try to give you the time you need, but I don't know if I can." His voice was suddenly harsh. "I'm hurting too, dammit."

She watched the door close behind him with stunned disbelief. He meant it. She heard the muffled sound of his voice through the closed door. He must be telephoning his blasted orders for her restriction right now. Within fifteen minutes the entire place would be bristling with guards.

She felt fury surge through her. Well, she wouldn't be here in fifteen minutes. She'd have to leave the suitcase. She ran to the bureau and grabbed up her passport and wallet and jammed them into the back pockets of her jeans. Then she was out on the balcony, climbing over the balustrade. It was only a six- or seven-foot drop to the courtyard below and, by lowering herself with her hands until she hung full length, she lessened the jump to only a few feet.

Then she was running across the courtyard in the direction of the stables.

TEN

OEDIPUS WAS ON the far side of the pasture when she climbed the fence. Trust him to make a difficult situation worse. She had hoped he would be close enough so that she could just jump on him and be out the gate in a matter of seconds. Now she would have to run across the pasture and hope he wouldn't spook and leave her to chase after him.

She leaped down and streaked across the pasture toward the stallion. "Oedipus," she called softly. "It's only me. You don't want to run away. We're a team, remember? Why don't you come over here and we'll go for a ride?"

He was ignoring her. Maybe that wasn't all bad. At least he didn't appear to be skittish today.

"Stay away from him, Pandora."

Philip! Her pace faltered as she glanced over her shoulder. He was swiftly climbing the fence, his expression as dark as his voice was menacing.

Oh, let Oedipus be good today. There wasn't time for his usual shenanigans. She was next to him now and with one spring was on his back. He half reared and her knees gripped him firmly. "Not now, boy. Please."

He wasn't listening. He went through a series of bucks that would have done justice to a rodeo bronco and finished with a rear that almost toppled them.

"Get off him." Philip was right in front of them. His blue-green eyes were blazing. "Get off him, dammit."

"No!" She glared down at him. "I'm leaving here. I'll send him back when I get someplace where I can find other transportation."

"In Sedikhan?" He shook his head. "I'll close the borders, if necessary, to keep you here."

"Then I'll ride him over the hills to Said Ababa." She smiled at him recklessly. "They don't like either you or Ben Raschid any too well. Perhaps they'll give me sanctuary." Oedipus began to rear again, and she had all she could do to stay on his back for the next minute or so. "Now get out of my way."

"And if you run into those bandits that are holed up in the hills there's a good chance you'll be raped or murdered," he said grimly, starting toward her again.

She felt Oedipus's muscles tense beneath her, and a sudden fear pierced the haze of fury that enveloped her. "No! Stay back. Oedipus—"

It was too late. Oedipus reared, his front hoofs flying, and Philip was right in front of those hoofs. She heard a low cry that chilled her blood.

"Philip!" She saw the blood on his temple and screamed. "No!" She was off Oedipus in an instant. At least Philip hadn't fallen to the ground. Perhaps the blow hadn't been too severe. She was by his side, her eyes enormous with fear as she saw the trickle of blood running down his cheek from the wound in his temple. "Are you all right?"

"No, I'm not all right," he bit out. "I'm mad as hell, frustrated, and I will probably have a colossal headache, thanks to our old friend Oedipus." He suddenly picked her up and slung her face down over his shoulder. "And you. Now try to refrain from struggling or I'll tie you up and gag you."

She felt a brief surge of indignation that was immediately submerged by a relief so intense that it made her go limp. Philip couldn't be badly hurt if he was able to carry her like this.

"Open that gate, blast it!"

She heard a low exclamation and then she was being carried through the gate and across the stableyard. Her hair had tumbled forward over her eyes so that she had only brief glimpses of the stableboys and trainers as they passed, but she heard the low comments and laughter. Comments that didn't put her in any better temper.

"You can put me down now. Surrounded by all these chauvinistic idiots, I doubt I'll be able to escape. This isn't at all dignified."

"Since when has dignity ever mattered to you? I'm not letting you go until I have you in a place where you can't run away from me." They were abruptly out of the sun. The dirt of the stableyard had been replaced by the wooden planks and saw- dust of the stable itself. "Get out of here," he or- dered someone who was beyond her vision. "And stay out. Lock the stable doors behind you and don't open them until I tell you."

A pair of scuffed brown boots crossed her line of vision, and then the barn became suddenly dusky as the door was slammed shut.

She heard the bolt being shot as Philip moved down the line of stalls. "Don't you think you've car- ried this far enough?" she asked. "I'm getting dizzy from being upside down."

"Well, I've certainly carried you far enough." He knelt in an empty stall and put her down on a bed of fresh hay. "I'm getting a little dizzy myself."

"Are you?" She sat up, her face concerned. "You're still bleeding. Why did you have to be so stupid? You knew Oedipus wouldn't put up with being approached like that." She scrambled to her knees. "Let me look at it."

"It was the only way to get you off that contrary devil before he bucked you off." He reached into his back pocket, pulled out a white handkerchief, and dabbed carelessly at his cheek and temple. "You obviously weren't going to display any sense in the matter."

"Let me do that." She took the handkerchief and carefully wiped the blood away from the cut. It wasn't much more than a scratch she noticed with relief. Oedipus must have clipped him with the edge of his hoof. "You didn't have to try to commit suicide. You could have let me go."

"Never again," he said quietly. "Not as long as we both live."

"Which won't be very long for you if you continue to do crazy things like that," she said huskily. She felt as if something inside her was loosening, breaking up like an ice floe in sunlight. She had to blink rapidly to keep back the tears. "You could have had your brains knocked out, dammit."

"No loss. I don't seem to have many left since

you reappeared in my life." He closed his eyes, and his voice lowered. "Lord, you scared me. I thought he was going to throw you again." He was shaking, she realized incredulously. The trembling was barely perceptible, but it was there, nonetheless. He opened his eyes, and they were unutterably weary. "Please, don't do that to me again. I kept seeing you lying on that path in the hills, crumpled up like a broken doll. It was like repeating a nightmare."

Please. When had she ever heard Philip plead for anything? She tried desperately to hold on to her anger. "It was your fault. Who ever heard of anybody locking up a wife in this day and age?"

"You wouldn't stay," he said simply. "I can't do without you now."

"You mean you can't do without your child," she said dully.

"I know what I mean. What do I have to do to convince you? Shall I arrange for an abortion?"

"No!" Her eyes widened in shock. "You wouldn't do that."

"No. We'd end up hating each other if I did. Besides, that child is probably more alive to me than it is to you. I've had more time to think about it. I want that child, Pandora."

"I know that," she said shakily.

"I want it," he said slowly. "But I'll give it up. If you'll promise to stay with me for the next year, I'll relinquish all claim to the baby. Should you choose to leave me after that time, the child goes with you."

She froze. "You'd do that?"

"If I have to." A muscle jerked in his cheek. "I'm hoping that at the end of that year I will have been able to convince you to stay with me." He drew a deep, shuddering breath. "God, I hope that."

"Why?" she asked. "It's not like you. I can't believe you'd calmly give up your own child."

His lips twisted in a travesty of a smile. "Not calmly. Rebelliously, agonizingly, perhaps. But never calmly."

"Why?" she asked again, her voice a mere whisper.

"Because I love you." His hands came up to clasp her shoulders. "How many times do I have to tell you before you believe me?" There was a touch of desperation in his tone. "Yes, I want the baby. But only because it's your baby, not because it's mine. Because I know I'll love your child almost as much as I love you."

Hope leaped wildly. She moistened her lips. "I'm afraid to trust you."

"How long am I going to have to pay for that night? I know I hurt you. I know I can't turn back the clock. Look, would it help if I told you why I brought Natalie here?"

"I know why you brought her here. You wanted to get rid of me." Her lips were suddenly trembling. "You wanted to hurt me."

"Yes, I wanted to hurt you. I reacted like a madman when you told me you were leaving me." He was silent for a few seconds, gathering himself to go on. "I don't like being this vulnerable. God, I don't want to put it into words."

"Put what into words?"

"It was one of the games she used to play," he burst out. "Most of the time she wasn't very subtle in her little cruelties, but she enjoyed that one very much. I was an exceptionally lonely child. She made

sure of that. Lonely children are desperate for affection, and it was a weapon she could use. She was always trying to get back at my father through me."

"Helena Lavade," Pandora murmured. It was a
statement, not a question.

"Who else, but my charming mother? And she
could be very charming. She had been trained from
childhood to dazzle and please. I was an easy mark
for someone with her particular talents. When it
amused her she would spend a week or so lavishing
all her attention on me. I lapped it up like a starving
puppy."

She couldn't stand to see the pain and self-disgust
in his eyes. "Don't." She lifted a finger to his lips. "I
don't want to hear any more."

He took her hand from his mouth. "And I don't
want to say any more," he said. "But I will. I owe it
to you to bleed a little." He looked down at her
hand and began to play absently with her fingers.
"She liked Paris and Vienna and London. They
suited her expensive tastes, and it was easier to
elude my father in a large city. She always had a
lover in tow, and when she decided I was primed for

the kill, she would tell me that she was going away with him. She'd smile very sweetly and tell me I mustn't ever expect her to stay. She told me I was too boring to keep her amused for very long." His hand closed on hers with convulsive force. "I can remember begging her to stay, but she would only laugh."

Stay, he had said as he'd held Pandora in his arms last night. Stay forever. Her throat tightened with an aching tenderness.

"I didn't think that morning you told me you were going to Paris, I just reacted," he said quietly. "You were leaving me, and I knew I already loved you a thousand times more than that bitch who gave birth to me. You had made me love you, and now you were leaving too."

"But you knew I loved you." She was trying to keep her voice from breaking. "I've always loved you."

His gaze lifted from her hand to her eyes. "I didn't believe it could ever really exist. Not for me. It was safer not to believe than to be hurt again." He moved his shoulders in a shrug. "Now you've heard my little confession," he said with a touch of self-mockery. "I hope you listened closely, for I never intend to indulge in that maudlin form of self-pity again."

"You won't have to," she said gently. "You didn't have to confess anything to me."

"Yes, I did." There was no bitterness now in the smile he gave her. It contained only tenderness and a little sadness. "You said you didn't trust me. It's very difficult to trust without understanding. Ask me. I'm the expert on cynicism." He lifted her hand to his lips and kissed her palm. "Until now."

"You mean it?" she asked, her eyes bright with tears. "Oh, please mean it, Philip."

"I mean it." The words were as solemn as a vow. "I never meant anything more in my life. Do you remember when we were on the cliff that morning and I told you what miracles could come from such an ordinary source as water?"

" 'One pure, crystal drop of water and the desert blooms,' " she quoted softly.

"I was like that desert until you came into my life. Barren and eroding into nothingness." He smiled. "I didn't even know it. That's the most dangerous kind of erosion, the kind that can't be detected until it's too late. Then you came and bubbled through that desert like a clear, deep stream. You brought me to life again."

She drew a deep breath, struggling to keep the incredible happiness bursting inside her under control. "I've never been compared to an irrigation project before. Trust you to be different."

His lips moved from her palm to her wrist. "You want something more picturesque?" He met her eyes with a teasing glance. "I'll be glad to oblige. How about spring? I hate to be cast as the god of the underworld when I'm trying to impress you with my more noble qualities, but you certainly fit the role of Persephone. You bring the spring, Pandora. Every minute of every day you bring the warmth and the sunlight and the blossoming to my winter world." His voice lowered to a husky whisper. "Please, don't take away that spring."

Beautiful. Had any man ever spoken such beautiful words to a woman before? The tears that had been brimming in her eyes could no longer be contained. Two drops ran slowly down her cheeks. "I wish you'd make up your mind. First you're a desert and then you're Pluto. A girl could get confused."

"I'm nothing but a man," he said gently. "Just a man who wants to share your life. Who wants to be your friend and your lover and the father of your child. Is that clear enough?"

"Oh, Philip." She flew into his arms, hugging him as tightly as she could. "You know that's not true. You're Hannibal and Alexander and a Khadim and..." She ran out of words. "Oh, just everything."

His arms went around her. "Am I?" he asked huskily. "That's nice to know." Then, with the half-mocking arrogance that was quintessentially Philip, he added, "I suspected as much, of course, but it's always good to have one's qualities appreciated." His hand was stroking her hair with infinite gentleness. "You'll stay with me?"

"I'll stay." The words were muffled in the front of his shirt. "You'd have to tie me up and ship me out of Sedikhan in a trunk to get rid of me now."

"I don't think that's likely." His chuckle reverberated against her ear. "I'm already regarded as something of a barbarian in diplomatic circles, but even I draw the line somewhere. Besides, the cramped position might be bad for the baby."

"The baby." She pulled back to look up at him, her face lighting up. "I'm going to have a baby. Isn't that wonderful?"

"Very wonderful," he agreed. "You act as if that fact has just come home to you. If you recall, that's what this hullabaloo is all about."

"It *has* just come home. All I could feel was hurt and anger and betrayal when my father told me I was pregnant and that you knew all along." Her hands abruptly tightened on his shoulders. "My Lord, what if I'd taken another fall off Oedipus and hurt the baby?"

"You didn't fall," he said gently. "It didn't happen. Stop worrying about it."

She was gnawing at her lower lip. "But it could have happened. How irresponsible can you get? I suppose I'll have to stop riding right away."

"We'll bring in an obstetrician and see what he

recommends." Philip's lips tightened. "But there's no way you'll get on Oedipus again."

"All right, I won't," she said meekly. Her lashes lowered to hide the mischief in her eyes. "Until after the baby's born."

"Pandora!"

She laughed. "He likes me," she protested laughingly. "He likes both of us. If he hadn't acted up today, it would have taken us much longer to get everything ironed out."

"You're casting that black devil in the role of Cupid?" Philip asked.

"Well, not exactly. It was very naughty of him to rear up and hit you with his hoof." She frowned. "We should really go back to the first-aid room so I can put some antiseptic on that cut."

"Presently." He pressed her back on the mound of hay and settled down beside her. "Why don't we just lie still and relax for a while? I like it here."

So did she. The dusky half light of the stable was so beautifully intimate and the hay beneath them was soft and springy, the scent both clean and sweet. Philip's long, lean body was warm and hard and infinitely dear as he folded her more closely against him.

She cuddled contentedly, her cheek finding the hollow of his shoulder. "All right, for just a little while." She suddenly chuckled. "What do you suppose the stableboys are thinking out there? After the way you carried me in here, they're probably expecting to hear screams and the sound of a horse-whip."

His lips twisted in a rueful smile. "My screams, more than likely. Most of them know what a wild-cat you are. When that guard saw you hanging from the balcony he phoned me rather than run after you himself. I'm surprised none of them offered to stay and protect me."

"I'll protect you," she said dreamily. "You won't need anyone else. I'll take such good care of you."

His lips took hers in a kiss of enchanting sweetness that opened entire new horizons of joy and commitment. How wonderful that so much could be contained in just a single kiss.

"And I'll take care of you," he said with a touch of huskiness in his voice. "Now, hush. I want to lie here and hold you and be peaceful for a bit. Heaven knows, I'll get little enough chance to do it in the future."

"Will you mind?"

"No, I won't mind. You expect a little discomfort when your life is starting to grow and change." He smiled. "You expect it, and you look forward to it."

Growth and change. Such exciting words for what was to come. Growing individually, yet together, sharing ideas and experiences. Sharing love. A love that would make their lives rich and fertile for the blossoming to come.

"What are you thinking about?" he asked curiously, gazing down into her glowing face.

She laughed softly. "Deserts," she said. "And blossoms." Her expression held all the wonder and eagerness of a child. "Oh, Philip, we have so many wonderfully exciting things in store for us. I can hardly wait!"

His eyes were intent and warmly tender. "Neither can I." He kissed her gently on the forehead. "Neither can I, love."

The never-before-published sequel

The Treasure

Available now

Read on for a sneak peak
of THE TREASURE . . .

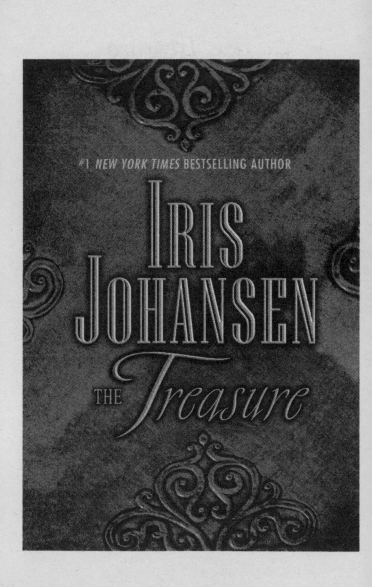

IRIS JOHANSEN

THE *Treasure*

The Treasure
Available now

HIS POWER WAS WANING, fading like that blood-red sun setting behind the mountains.

Jabbar Al Nasim's fists clenched with fury as he gazed out at the sun sinking on the horizon. It should not be. It made no sense that he should be so afflicted. Weakness was for those other fools, not for him.

Yet he had always known it would come. It had even come for Sinan, the Old Man of the Mountain. But he had always been stronger than the old man in both mind and spirit. Sinan had bent before the yoke, but Nasim had prepared for it.

Kadar.

"You sent for me, master?"

He turned to see Ali Balkir striding along the battlements toward him. The man's voice was soft, hesitant, and he could see the fear in his face. Nasim felt a jolt of fierce pleasure as he realized the captain had not detected any loss of power. Well, why should he? Nasim had always been master here, in spite of what outsiders thought. Sinan might have been the King of Assassins, feared by kings and warriors alike, but Nasim had been the one who had guided his footsteps. Everyone here at the fortress knew and groveled at his feet.

And they'd continue to grovel. He would not let this monstrous thing happen to him.

Balkir took a hurried step back as he saw Nasim's expression. "Perhaps I was mistaken. I beg your forgiveness for intrud—"

"No, stay. I have a task for you."

Balkir drew a relieved breath. "Another attack on the Frankish ships? Gladly. I brought you much gold from my last journey. I will bring you even more this—"

"Be silent. I wish you to return to Scotland where you left Kadar Ben Arnaud and the foreigners. You are to tell him nothing of what has transpired here. Do not mention me. Tell him only that Sinan is claiming his price. Bring him to me."

Balkir's eyes widened. "Sinan? But Sinan is—"

"Do you question me?"

"No, never." Balkir moistened his lips. "But what if he refuses?"

Balkir was terrified, Nasim realized, and not of failing him. Nasim had forgotten that Balkir was at the fortress at the time Kadar underwent his training; Balkir knew how adept Kadar was in all the dark arts. More adept than any man Nasim had ever known, and Kadar was only a boy of ten and four when he came to the mountain. How proud Sinan had been of him. What plans he had made for the two of them. He had never realized Nasim had plans of his own for Kadar.

All wasted when Kadar had left the dark path and rejected Sinan to live with the foreigners. What a fool the Old Man had been to let him go.

But it was not too late. What Sinan had lost, Nasim could reclaim.

If Kadar did not die as the others had died.

Well, if he died, he died. Kadar was only a man; it was the power that was important.

"He won't refuse," Nasim said. "He gave Sinan his word in exchange for the lives of the foreigners."

"What if he does?"

"You *are* questioning me," Nasim said with dangerous softness.

Balkir turned pale. "No, master. Of course he won't refuse. Not if you say he won't. I only—"

"Be gone." Nasim waved his hand. "Set sail at once."

Balkir nodded jerkily and backed away from him. "I will bring him. Whether or not he wishes to come I will force—"

The words cut off abruptly as Nasim turned his back on him. The man was only trying to gain respect in his eyes. He would have no more chance against Kadar if he tried to use force than he would against Nasim, and he probably knew it.

But he wouldn't have to use force. Kadar would come. Not only because of his promise but because he would know what would result if he didn't. Sinan had spared the lives of Lord Ware, his woman, Thea, and the child Selene and given them all a new life in Scotland. Nasim had permitted the foolishness because he had wanted to keep Kadar safe until it was time to use him.

But no one would be more aware than Kadar that the safety Sinan had given could always be taken away.

Kadar had shown a baffling softness toward his friend Lord Ware and a stranger bond with the child Selene. Such emotions were common on the bright path, but Nasim had taught Kadar better. It seemed fitting that he be caught in his master's noose because he'd ignored his teachings.

The fortress gate was opening and Balkir rode through it. He kicked his horse into a dead run down the mountain. He would be in Hafir in a few days and set sail as soon as he could stock his ship, the *Dark Star*.

Nasim turned back to the setting sun. It had descended almost below the horizon now, darkness was closing in. But it would return tomorrow, blasting all before it with its power.

And so would Nasim.

His gaze shifted north toward the sea. Kadar was across that sea in that cold land of Scotland, playing at being one of them, the fools, the bright ones. But it would be just a matter of months before he would be here. Nasim had waited five years. He could wait a little longer. Yet an odd eagerness was beginning to replace his rage and desperation. He wanted him here *now*.

He felt the power rising within him and he closed his eyes and sent the call forth.

"Kadar."

"SHE'S BEING VERY FOOLISH." Thea frowned as she watched Selene across the great hall. "I don't like this, Ware."

"Neither does Kadar," Ware said cheerfully as he took a sip of his wine. "I'm rather enjoying it. It's interesting to see our cool Kadar disconcerted."

"Will it also be interesting if Kadar decides to slaughter that poor man at whom she's smiling?" Thea asked tartly. "Or Lord Kenneth, who she partnered in the last country dance?"

"Yes." He smiled teasingly at her. "It's been far too peaceful here for the last few years. I could use a little diversion."

"Blood and war are not diversions except to warriors like you." Her frown deepened. "And I thought you very happy here at Montdhu. You did not complain."

He lifted her hand and kissed the palm. "How would I dare with such a termagant of a wife."

"Don't tease. Have you been unhappy?"

"Only when you robbed me of craftsmen for my castle so that you could have them build a ship for your silk trade."

"I needed that ship. What good is it to produce fine silks if you can't sell them? It wasn't sensible to—" She shook her head. "You know I was right, and you have your castle now. It's as fine and strong as you could want. Everyone at the feast tonight has told you they have never seen a more secure fortress."

His smile faded. "And we might well have need of our fortress soon."

She frowned. "Have you heard news from the Holy Land?"

He shook his head. "But we walk a fine line, Thea. We've been lucky to have these years to prepare."

Ware was still looking over his shoulder, Thea thought sadly. Well, who could blame him? They had fled the wrath of the Knights Templar to come to this land, and if the Knights found out that Ware was not dead, as they thought, they would be unrelenting in their persecution. Ware and Thea had almost been captured before their journey started. It had been Kadar who had bargained with Sinan, the head of the assassins, to lend them a ship to take them to Scotland. But that was the past, and Thea would not have Ware moody tonight when he had so much to celebrate.

"We're not lucky, we're intelligent. And the Knights Templar are foolish beyond belief if they think you would betray them. It makes me angry every time I think of it. Now drink your wine and enjoy this evening. We've made a new life and everything is fine."

He lifted his cup. "Then why are you letting the fact that your sister is smiling prettily at Lord Douglas upset you?"

"Because Kadar hasn't taken his eyes off her all evening." Her gaze returned to her sister. Selene's pale-gold silk gown made her dark red hair glow with hidden fires, and her green eyes shone with vitality—and recklessness. The little devil knew exactly what she was doing, Thea thought crossly. Selene was impulsive at times, but this was not such an occasion. Her every action tonight was meant to provoke Kadar. "And I didn't invite the entire countryside to see your splendid new castle so that she could expose them to mayhem."

"Tell her. Selene loves you. She won't want you unhappy."

"I will." She rose to her feet and strode down the hall toward the great hearth, before which Selene was holding court. Ware was right: Selene might be willful, but she had a tender heart. She would never intentionally hurt anyone she loved. All Thea had to do was confront her sister, express her distress, and the problem would be solved.

Maybe.

"Don't stop her, Thea."

She glanced over her shoulder to see Kadar behind her.

He had been leaning against the far pillar only seconds ago, but she was accustomed to the swift silence of his movements.

"Stop her?" She smiled. "I don't know what you mean."

"And don't lie to me either." Kadar's lips tightened. "I'm a little too bad-tempered tonight to deal in pretense." He took her arm and led her toward the nearest corner of the hall. "And you've never done it well. You're burdened with a pure and honest soul."

"And I suppose you're the devil himself."

He smiled. "Only a disciple."

"Nonsense."

"Well, perhaps only half devil. I've never been able to convince you of my sinful character. You never wanted to see that side of me."

"You're kind and generous and our very dear friend."

"Oh, yes, which proves what good judgment you have."

"And arrogant, stubborn, and with no sense of humility."

He inclined his head. "But I've the virtue of patience, my lady, which should outweigh all my other vices."

"Stop mocking." She turned to face him. "You're angry with Selene."

"Am I?"

"You know you are. You've been watching her all evening."

"And you've been watching me." One side of his lips lifted in a half smile. "I was wondering whether you'd decide to attack me or Selene."

"I have no intention of attacking anyone." She stared directly into his eyes. "Do you?"

"Not at the moment. I've just told you how patient I am."

Relief surged through her. "She doesn't mean anything. She's just amusing herself."

"She means something." He glanced back toward the hearth. "She means to torment and hurt me and drive me to the edge." His tone was without expression. "She does it very well, doesn't she?"

"It's your fault. Why don't you offer for her? You know Ware and I have wanted the two of you to wed for this past year. Selene is ten and seven. It's past time she had a husband."

"I'm flattered you'd consider a humble bastard like myself worthy of her."

"You are not flattered. You know your own worth."

"Of course, but the world would say it was a poor match. Selene is a lady of a fine house now."

"Only because you helped us escape from the Holy Land and start again. Selene was a slave in the House of Nicholas and only a child when you bought her freedom as a favor to me. She was destined to spend her life embroidering his splendid silks and being given to his customers for their pleasure. You saved her, Kadar. Do you think she would ever look at another man if you let her come close to you?"

"Don't interfere, Thea."

"I *will* interfere. You know better. She's worshipped you since she was a child of eleven."

"Worship? She's never worshipped me. She knows me

too well." He smiled. "You may not believe in my devilish qualities, but she does. She's always known what I am. Just as I've always known what she is."

"She's a hardworking, honest, loving woman who needs a husband."

"She's more than that. She's extraordinary, the light in my darkness. And she's still not ready for me."

"Ready? Most women her age have children already."

"Most women haven't suffered as she suffered. It scarred her. I can wait until she heals."

"But can she?" Thea glanced toward the hearth again. Oh, God, Selene was no longer there.

"It's all right. She and Lord Douglas just left the hall and went out into the courtyard."

How had he known that? Sometimes it seemed Kadar had eyes in the back of his head.

"Kadar, don't—"

He bowed. "If you'll excuse me, I'll go and bring her back."

"Kadar, I *won't* have violence this night."

"Don't worry, I won't shed blood on the fine new rushes you put down on the floor." He moved toward the courtyard. "But the stones of the courtyard wash up quite nicely."

"Kadar!"

"Don't follow me, Thea." His voice was soft but inflexible. "Stay out of it. This is what she wants, what she's tried to goad me to all evening. Don't you realize that?"

Where was Kadar? Selene wondered impatiently. She had been out here a good five minutes and he still hadn't appeared. She didn't know how long she could keep Lord Douglas from taking her back to the hall. He was a boring, stodgy young man and had been shocked when she'd suggested going out to the courtyard. "It's a fine night. I do feel much better now that I've had a breath of air."

Lord Douglas looked uneasy. "Then perhaps we should go back inside. Lord Ware would not like us being out here alone. It's not fitting."

"In a moment." Where *was* he? She had felt his gaze on her all evening. He would have seen—

"The Saracen was watching us," Lord Douglas said. "I'm sure he will tell Lord Ware."

"Saracen?" Her gaze flew to his face. "What Saracen?"

"Kadar Ben Arnaud. Isn't he a Saracen? That's what they call him."

"Who are 'they'?"

He shrugged. "Everyone."

"Kadar's mother was Armenian, his father a Frank."

He nodded. "A Saracen."

She should be amused that he had put Kadar, who could never be labeled, in a tight little niche. She was not amused. She fiercely resented the faint patronizing note in his voice. "Why not call him a Frank like his father? Why a Saracen?"

"He just seems . . . He's not like us."

No more than a panther was like a sheep or a glittering diamond like a moss-covered rock, she thought furiously. "Kadar belongs here. My sister and her husband regard him as a brother."

"Surely not." He looked faintly shocked. "Though I'm sure he's good at what he does. These Saracens are supposed to be fine seamen, and he does your silk trading, doesn't he?"

She wanted to slap him. "Kadar does more than captain our ship. He's a part of Montdhu. We're proud and fortunate to have him here."

"I didn't mean to make you—"

She lost track of what he was saying.

Kadar was coming.

She had known he would follow her, but Selene still smothered a leap of excitement as she caught sight of him in the doorway. He was moving slowly, deliberately, almost leisurely down the stairs. This was not good. That wasn't the response she wanted from him. She took a step closer to Lord Douglas and swayed. "I believe I still feel a little faint."

He instinctively put a hand on her shoulder to steady her. "Perhaps I should call the lady Thea."

"No, just stay—"

"Good evening, Lord Douglas." Kadar was coming toward them. "I believe it's a little cool out here for Selene. Why don't you go fetch her cloak?"

"We were just going in," Lord Douglas said quickly. "Lady Selene felt a little faint and we—"

"Faint?" Kadar's brows lifted as he paused beside them. "She appears quite robust to me."

He's not like us, Douglas had said.

No, he wasn't like any of these men who had come to honor Ware tonight. He was like no one Selene had ever met. Now, standing next to heavyset, red-faced Lord Douglas, the differences were glaringly apparent. Kadar's dark eyes dominated a bronze, comely face that could reflect both humor and intelligence. He was tall, his powerful body deceptively lean, with a grace and confidence the other man lacked. But the differences were not only on the surface. Kadar was as deep and unfathomable as the night sky, and it was no wonder these simple fools could not understand how exceptional he was.

"She was ill," Lord Douglas repeated.

"But I'm sure she feels better now." Kadar paused. "So you may remove your hand from her shoulder."

Selene felt a surge of fierce satisfaction. This was better. Kadar's tone was soft, but so was the growl of a tiger before it pounced.

Evidently Lord Douglas didn't miss the threat. He snatched his hand away as if burned. "She was afraid she would—"

"Selene is afraid of nothing." He smiled at Selene. "Though she should be."